PARIAH

And Other Stories

PARIAH

And Other Stories

by Joan Williams

An Atlantic Monthly Press Book

Little, Brown and Company   Boston/Toronto

10/1983
gen'l

FIRST EDITION

The following stories have been previously published:
"Rain Later," in *Mademoiselle*; "The Morning and the Eve-
ning," in *The Atlantic Monthly*; "No Love for the Lonely" and
"Going Ahead," in the *Saturday Evening Post*; "Pariah," in
McCall's; "Spring Is Now," in *The Virginia Quarterly Review*;
"Jesse," in *Esquire*; "Vistas" (as "An Invitation to Lunch"), in
the *Westport* (Conn.) *News*.
"The Morning and the Evening" and "The Sound of Si-
lence" appeared in slightly different form in Joan Williams's
novel *The Morning and the Evening*.

Library of Congress Cataloging in Publication Data
Williams, Joan, 1928–
    Pariah.
    "An Atlantic Monthly Press Book."
    Contents: Rain later — The morning and the evening
— The sound of silence — No love for the lonely — [etc.]
    I. Title.
PS3573.l4494P3   1983   813'.54   83-1002
ISBN 0-316-94233-2

ATLANTIC–LITTLE, BROWN BOOKS
ARE PUBLISHED BY
LITTLE, BROWN AND COMPANY
IN ASSOCIATION WITH
THE ATLANTIC MONTHLY PRESS

BP
Designed by Dede Cummings

Published simultaneously in Canada
by Little, Brown & Company (Canada) Limited

PRINTED IN THE UNITED STATES OF AMERICA

In memory of William Faulkner
(1897-1962)

Contents

Rain Later

*A*RVENIA stood for a moment looking beyond where the garden ended at the back of the house. Squinting her eyes at the distant muddy gullies, she moved her hands, without thinking, to pull open the screen door in front of her. Its sagging heaviness had scraped a white pattern into the worn darkness of the wooden floor and it screeched over this now and stuck halfway at a swollen notch. Arvenia gave the door a kick and flung it backward against the screened side of the porch, snapping the door's coiled hinge.

She looked down then and hooked the hinge back into place, balancing in her other hand two great hunks of warm yellowish corn bread. These she threw out into the mud, to the two hound dogs who had slunk from beneath the house. The dogs gulped them down and then stood watching her, their sad brown eyes rolling up into their red sockets, but Arvenia pushed the door to and said, "Git, dawg." Then, leaning her head against the dirty screen, she said softly, "I'm tired, I'm tired, I'm tired, dear God, I'm tired." And above the gullies the sky was darkening as if there would be more rain.

A skinny chicken pecked angrily at a tomato peeling washed into the deep mud around the steps, and one of the dogs lunged at the bird, growling to himself. The chicken flew crookedly, squawking, over the fence, into the garden, and Arvenia banged against the screen and yelled, "Dawg, dawg, aren't they skinny enough now?"

She turned to go back into the house and ran into a big tin oil drum almost overflowing with a floating mixture of peelings and scraps. It was the mealy smell of this that had been mingling with the rainy chicken-spattered smell of the backyard. "Mag, I thought Albert was coming to feed those pigs," she called.

"That good-for-nuthin' nigger ain't gonna do nuthin', Miz Arvy. I tol' him and tol' him come take that stuff." The voice from the kitchen rose unhurriedly over the movings of pans. Arvenia glanced over her shoulder again and then moved from the outdoor light into the warm partial darkness of the kitchen. "I'm fixin' to leave him, he don't do somethin' soon. Ain't done a lick of work since they stopped pickin' cotton down to Mista Johnson's. Not narrin a lick." The black face was shiny over the hulk of iron stove into which Mag was sticking wads of paper and dried corncobs.

"You'd be better off," Arvenia said.

"Sho' is the truth." Mag answered. "What I'm to fix for dinner?"

"Fix the chicken," Arvenia told her. "Emily and Jeanie are comin' down from Memphis, and you know Emily always says to have chicken when she comes because she can't ever fix it at home as good as we have it."

A big slow grin covered Mag's face. "Lawd," she mused, "I still can't believe Miss Emily's grown and married and got a baby. It seems only a while she was a baby herself and me carryin' her around." Arvenia got up from the table where she had been tightening the caps on the jars of canned to-

[4]

matoes and beans lined up there. Yes, she thought, only a
while. She dried her hands, and for a moment the plain gold
band on her finger almost shone. She glanced at it as though
seeing it for the first time in a long time, noticing all the
scratches. I used to be so careful of it, she remembered. But
it didn't really matter anymore. Jim Acree had been dead for
so long.

"They don't come back so often, do they, Miz Arvy?" the
Negro asked. Suddenly it didn't seem like only a while, and
she felt very tired and leaned against the sink.

"No, they don't come back so often, Mag," Arvenia answered. "They forget, and their children forget, or just don't
care." Much to Arvenia's surprise, her voice caught.

"Yes'm, seems like it," the Negro answered quickly and
turned her back, dipping her heavy arms into a pan of dish-
water. The water splashed up and left slow suds running
from her elbows down to her whitish wrists and into the water
again. She looked down into the pan hard, for she was afraid
the white woman was going to cry. Maybe. Arvenia straightened the jars into precise rows and then into precise rows
again, moving them smoothly over the oilcloth.

Finally she said, "It's ten o'clock, Mag, and I'm going to
take a nap. Ever think you'd see the day I went to bed in the
middle of the morning?"

"No'm," Mag answered her, "but you go take one. Ain't
nothin' wrong with that. Lots of folks don't even get up till
ten o'clock." The dishes rattled more slowly and the suds
were not so frequent up and down her arms. They stopped
finally.

The bed creaked with Arvenia's weight, and she lay back
slowly, feeling its yielding to the places of her body and the

pillow soft and cold to her cheek. Things came to her mind, and she thought about them or pushed them away. She heard the sounds of the day go on without her, and it was pleasant not to be a part of them for a while. The iceman came to the porch. Mag went out, talking to him in low soft tones, and he answered her in the same ones, their words so quick together as to be almost unintelligible.

Down the road, after the iceman's truck had made the usual car noises pulling away, came a passing whistle. Jimmy on his way home from town, she thought. He might stop in, but he won't. I'd have to get up if he came in. One grandchild right down the road and passes by every day. Of course he comes in sometimes, and then wouldn't it be silly if he dropped in every time he passed by? What would we say to each other so many times?

Two car doors slammed, and steps ran and steps walked on the front porch. She raised herself slightly and knew it was her daughter and granddaughter. I will get up. I am glad they are here, but I am very tired. It is almost an imposition that I have to get up. I think they will leave to go home about four, and then I can go back to bed again.

Then the child was there and threw her arms around her neck. "Granmuther," she said. And Arvenia felt the littleness of her, the tiny-boned arms for a moment soft around her, and slight pressure for a moment between the two. "Baby," she answered softly. Her daughter bent and touched her slightly on the cheek, and the old woman felt for a minute something like yearning, like desire to own her, to have the chance again to mold her. "Hello, Emily," she said. "I was beginning to worry you weren't coming."

"It's that awful road that slowed us down," her daughter said. "It's nothing but mud ruts from here to the highway.

[6]

Can't Uncle Bob or someone do something about it?" Arvenia smoothed out the wrinkles in the comfort where she had been lying down. "I don't know," she answered. "I haven't been anywhere and I haven't heard anyone else talking about it or complaining."

"I guess everybody is used to it." Emily seemed to be trying to excuse the road now. "But I think it's going to rain on it some more, so we'd better start back early or we'll never make it home."

Arvenia went to the south porch and looked at the sky. It was full of wisps of black clouds running through clear ones as though it couldn't make up its mind whether to rain or not. But it made the day darker than usual at this time; it was almost like dusk, and at dusk she could go to sleep again. She turned at the child's laughter. Jeanie ran in calling, "Momma, here's Mag," pulling the delighted Negro by the hand. Mag grinned all over.

"Mighty good to see you again, Miz Emily."

"It's good to see you — heavens, haven't you gotten your teeth yet?"

"Yes'm, I got 'em, but I just don't wear 'em. They bothers me too much." The colored woman laughed.

"You mean you spent all that money to get them and then you never wear them?"

Arvenia wondered why this should bother Emily so much. What difference should it make to her whether or not Mag wore her teeth? To Mag it evidently made not the slightest bit of difference. The child suddenly threw herself into the Negro's skirts, hugging her gleefully and crooning into the soft fatness. "Maggie, waggy, baggy, taggy," she laughed. "Will you show me the chickens," she asked, and Mag looked down and hugged her with happiness. "I sho' will, baby, soon as dinner is over."

Emily said, "Jeanie, let Mag alone. She has too much to do to be fooling with you."

"Oh, Mag had rather fool with Jeanie than fix dinner. You know that," Arvenia couldn't help saying. Why don't you let them alone? she wanted to scream.

Emily got up from the hard rocker in which she'd been sitting and went over to the mirror. She straightened her hair and ran a finger over her lipstick. Arvenia looked at her profile, at the line of her cheekbone, the eyebrow, nose. Exactly like Jim's, she thought. How can anyone forget when they have children to remind them? she wondered. And does one love the children perhaps because of something like that? She stood up and straightened her apron as though unconsciously letting fall a lapful of thoughts that she didn't want. "Mag, you better start dinner now," she called, and immediately the rich deep laughter and the thin tinkle of laughter that had been going on in the kitchen stopped.

Mag answered, "Yes'm." There was a flatness in her voice, just as there was a flatness in her lap, Arvenia knew, when she set the child down.

"I'll help you," she heard Jeanie say. Immediately Emily called out to her to stop bothering Mag. Arvenia wanted to say something again but she felt there was no use. She sat down again, and her mind settled a moment and wandered off onto the thoughts it had been shoving away ever since Emily had come. Let us please find some mutual ground, she wanted to say. I'm your mother and you shouldn't have to put on a mask with me. I want to love you and laugh and make up silly rhymes as we used to do. But she said none of this and sat in silent meditation wondering why she didn't say what she was thinking. With a start she realized that Emily had been staring at her and she felt afraid because Emily had seen her sitting like this, thinking so hard.

"Mother, what is it?" Emily asked softly, and it was as if for a moment there could be something there. Arvenia thought, I will say it. "Nothing," she answered, "but Emily —"

"Well then, for goodness' sake don't sit there looking like Whistler's Mother."

Arvenia leaned back and rested her head on the pillowed back of the chair, feeling against her neck the rough work of the crocheted doily. "I'm just tired today," she sighed.

"And no wonder, working the way you do — and for no reason. You've got Mag and Albert to do half the work you do yourself. It's ridiculous."

"What would I do, just sit?"

"You could find things to do that weren't actually farm work."

This could go on, Arvenia thought. There's no use going through it again. I just can't make her understand that I'd die if I didn't have work to do. From the time her father and I got married it was work. And now I can't change my ways. We worked so she wouldn't have to, and it's the thing that has drawn us apart. She can't understand my way, and I've never known hers. Arvenia watched her daughter again, unnaturally aware of her simple movements, sitting in the chair, rocking slowly. Had she and Jim done right? But it was too late now. Jeanie running in and climbing into her mother's lap interrupted the quietness. The two sat there talking while Arvenia went into the kitchen to see about the meal. It is funny, she thought — a mother can never really stop loving her child, or the child the mother, I don't believe. Even though something completely alien comes between.

Mag had sliced the tomatoes already, and there was really nothing for Arvenia to do. She carried the last dish in to the table and moved some of the silverware and straightened the napkins. All at once she felt tired again, and it was an effort to go to the door and call, "Dinner, Emily."

They sat in silence until Jeanie aroused a scolding for putting too much sugar in her tea. There was a silence again, and Arvenia said abruptly, "I haven't seen so much rain in years. Everybody's been talking about it."

Emily looked down into her plate. "Yes," she said, "and it still looks like it's going to rain again. We are really going to have to start back early."

Mag brought in chocolate cake and set the plate down before Arvenia. She took a small piece, but she didn't really want any. For some reason she thought for a moment of how chocolate cake would look in the rain. She watched Jeanie hold her cake tenderly in her hand, nibbling at the edges. Mag was still standing there. "Some folks are worried about whether the water's goin' to wash up over the levee," Mag said, her eyes thoughtful.

Arvenia spoke to her. "That's really going to be the ruination of the cotton, then. Albert won't do a lick of work."

Mag laughed outright. "That nigger don't do nothin' nohow, Miz Arvy." She went into the kitchen still chuckling to herself. The rush of water for the dishes almost drowned out her slow beginning to sing "Jesus, Jesus, I'm comin'."

They got up from the table and went back to the other room. Arvenia usually took a nap after lunch and she felt sleepy now even though she had rested in the morning. She wanted to take her nap now but she wouldn't since Emily had to leave so early.

Jeanie was pulling out the drawers in her sewing machine, building houses and things with the spools. I hope she puts them back, Arvenia thought. I'm her grandmother, after all; I could tell her to. But I probably won't. Emily sat in the hard rocker again, and Arvenia thought of asking her why she didn't sit in the soft one, but she changed her mind because somehow it seemed right for Emily to sit in the hard straight rocker. Emily stopped rocking and turned to Arvenia. "Momma, doesn't Albert ever do anything? Why don't you —"

"He does everything he's suppose' to do," Arvenia cut in quickly. For heaven's sake, for heaven's sake, is that what you've been sitting there thinking? Why do you worry about all these things? Emily began to rock back and forth in quick, short, hard rocks, which were the only kind you could rock in that chair. Her hands moved in little knottings together, and Arvenia felt she should have been knitting furiously. Mag came in, her apron wet-splashed, to take Jeanie out to see the chickens. The child jumped up hurriedly, scattering the spools under the bed, the chairs, table, everywhere.

Emily said, "Jeanie, come right back here and pick up those things before you go anywhere."

The child stopped, her face full of quick indecision.

"That's all right," Arvenia said, "you can pick them up later."

After the two went out the room was suddenly very quiet. That same quiet that Arvenia noticed other times. Just certain times the house was suddenly so quiet. Arvenia looked at Emily, who was still rocking and who looked back with something like a question on her face. It's as if she were saying, "Well, here we are, now what?" Arvenia thought.

"I went out and pulled you some tomatoes yesterday for you to take back with you. I'll get some beans this afternoon if it doesn't rain. It was so muddy yesterday I could hardly get in the garden."

"You shouldn't have gone out in so much wet, Mother."

"I've got a few shucks of corn, too."

"I'd like to have them, but I don't want you to go out in all that wet."

"I don't mind."

It seems it's after lunch and after dinner it gets so quiet, she thought, after she and Emily hadn't said any more for a while and just the rocking was the only sound. Footsteps sounded on the porch outside, and Arvenia got up quickly. She was glad someone was coming. It was a woman from down the road whom Arvenia knew only slightly because she had just moved there.

"Come in, come in," she called. And the woman unconsciously hurried her step a little, as though she felt a necessity for her presence quickly. So she came in with a feeling of having something important to do, and it bothered her because she couldn't quite think what it was.

"This is my daughter Emily. Down from Memphis. Miz Cooper who's just moved into the old Watkins place, Emily. You know where that is, don't you?"

"Yes, I used to play there when I was little. How're you, Miz Cooper? Do you like it here?"

"Fine, ma'am. I like it fairly much. Soon's we get straightened, that is. That's what I came down about, Miz Acree, to see if your nigger could split me some stove wood. My husband went off without doing it, and I don't feel like I should in my condition."

Both of the women noticed for the first time that she was slightly showing. "When's the baby coming?" Arvenia asked.

"Long about December. Is your nigger here?" the woman answered.

"December is a nice month. Jeanie came in August, didn't she, Emily? August is the worst month."

"Yes, it was August and I —"

"Is your nigger here?" the woman repeated.

[12]

"Oh, no, no he isn't here. But when he comes back I'll send him up to your place."

"Thank you. I'd appreciate that." The woman started for the door, and Arvenia followed her all the way out onto the porch. "Looks like more rain," she said.

The woman stopped and scanned the sky. "And pretty soon," she said. "I've never seen —"

"Well, I'll send the nigger up to you as soon as he comes back." Arvenia wanted her to go as much as she had been glad to see her. The woman realized now in half-thoughts why she had felt what she did when she came. She didn't understand what was expected of her. She felt uncertain and fumbled finding the door handle. Arvenia seemed to be staring at her. She wished she'd worn her other house-dress. She didn't know the woman from Memphis was here.

"Come back when you can stay for a time, Miz Cooper." Arvenia felt maybe she had been rude. She hoped Mrs. Cooper hadn't noticed.

"Thank you, I will," the woman answered. She went down the steps carefully, picking her way among the mud ruts. Arvenia stood looking after her, watching her slow progress down the road, watching her step here and then here and then there. She didn't realize how long she had stood there until Emily called to ask what she was doing. Arvenia went back inside and said, "Nothing." Emily was still sitting in the hard rocker, only she had stopped rocking and had turned the chair around so she was sitting facing the gullies. She looked out at them.

"We used to all play down on the old Watkins place, Momma, don't you remember? And once I went to sleep down in our playhouse and everyone was out searching for me. Don't you remember?"

"I don't know, seems like I do recall something like that."

"You must remember. You were so worried. Uncle Bob finally found me and then —"

"I believe I do remember." She didn't want to hear about that day. It made her tired to think back such a long time ago. "Isn't that Jeanie calling you?"

Emily went to the window and called to the child. Jeanie appeared at the bottom of the steps with a tiny puffy baby chicken peeping in her cupped hands. She raised her face to her mother.

"Mother, please do come see the baby chickens. I want to take one home. They are so cute."

"You aren't going to wag home a chicken. Put it down, it's got mites. Come in, we've got to go home."

Emily turned to face inside. "Seems like rain. We'd better start back."

Arvenia saw Jeanie set down the chick, which went running on little long legs frantically back to the peepings it heard. Jeanie looked after it.

"It ain't got mites," she said softly. "And I will so take one home sometime." She came up the steps heavily and kicked the door to with her foot. She went to the other door and stood waiting to go. I wish I could just give you one anyway, Arvenia thought. Emily was getting her things together, and Arvenia handed her the sack of tomatoes.

"I was going to get you some corn. Do you want to wait while I get it?"

"No, I don't need any." Emily took the sack as though she were afraid something was inside she didn't like. Arvenia regretted now she hadn't put the tomatoes in a cardboard box as she'd started to do. The sack seemed suddenly so dirty. She hadn't noticed before.

Jeanie put up her arms, and Arvenia felt again the slight

[14]

little pressure of her. The sweet warmness. Arvenia hugged her almost too hard. "Good-bye, Granmuther."

"Good-bye, baby, come to see Grandmother again soon." Her back hurt when she straightened up and she wanted to hurry inside and rest. She put her lips to her daughter's cheek.

"Good-bye, Emily, you all come whenever you can. I know you're busy at home, but I like to see you." Emily avoided her eyes.

"We will, Momma — it's hard to find just the right time, but we will."

They headed for the car in silence. The two of them, the child running ahead. Their heels sounded hollowly on the wooden porch. At the gate Arvenia stopped and put her arm around her daughter's waist lightly. She was sorry they had to go. It had been a rather short day after all. She hadn't had a chance to see Jeanie really. "Come again soon," she said again.

Emily smiled at her for a minute, giving her hand a small squeeze before walking on to the car. "We certainly will, Momma, as soon as we can, and you come up when you're able. We're always glad to have you."

"Good-bye."

"Good-bye."

The car started up slowly at first and then faster, kicking up dust as it went. The dust died down quickly, however, as if it knew that soon the rain would settle it anyway. Already the wind was getting cooler.

Arvenia went back into the house and began putting down the windows. She turned at Mag's footsteps. It was later then than she had realized and time for supper.

"They gone?"

"Yes."

"You still feelin' tired?"

"About the same."

"I'll fix yo' supper and then you go to bed." She went back to the kitchen.

Arvenia went to her room and picked up the spools. She put them all away and closed the drawers of the machine one by one. Then she sat down and rocked a little, just waiting for supper. She wasn't really hungry. Jimmy went by on his way home, whistling again. Mag came in softly in her shuffly old slippers and spoke as though to waken someone gently from sleep.

"Supper, Miz Arvy."

Arvenia slowly ate cold food left from noon. Mag did things about the kitchen, humming to herself. Arvenia rose and went to her room just as Mag began to sing the words again. "Jesus, Jesus, I'm comin'," she sang above the rattling of dishes. Arvenia sat listening to the sounds Mag made straightening up the kitchen. She heard her stop the water, ring out the cloth, hang up the dishpan. Everything was quiet for a moment, then Mag tiptoed in, whispered, "I'm gone, Miz Arvy."

Arvenia nodded her head and continued to rock. Mag returned to the kitchen, began gathering up her things. Arvenia got up and sat on the edge of the bed, then lay back slowly, easing out her back. She sighed a long sigh. Mag's heavy steps went across the porch. The door opened and closed softly, the steps creaked, and Mag was gone, singing her song again.

The house was so still, one of the quiet times, and Arvenia knew now that these happened when Mag left, when she was in the house alone. She wondered why she hadn't realized this before. She turned over and drew up a thin coverlet from the foot of the bed. A slight cool breeze was coming in the window and just then above the gullies there was a low grumble, and far off the rain started at last.

The Morning
and the Evening

𝒯HE owner-manager was also the ticket seller and ticket taker and would have been his own projectionist, too, if labor regulations had not forced him to hire a licensed one. He did not take his first customer for a loony and tried to charge him full admission.

The man next in line said quietly, "He don't usually pay but half fare."

The owner looked at his customer warily then; he did not look like a loony, was tall, thin, stoop-shouldered, with a weather-beaten face that seemed to know all about struggle and with eyes that looked as if he were thinking, even as if he were looking for something; they weren't empty, like the eyes of most loonies. The eyes were what fooled him.

He was hesitant: they might be trying to pull some kind of deal. You couldn't ever tell. He'd been taking his movie around in the back country for three years and didn't understand these people yet. Why'd they live in country like this, bother with the little they eked out of it?

Then the loony tried to say something, opened his mouth, and nothing came out except saliva. It drooled on his pink, hanging lip a minute, then ran down his chin and dropped onto his shirt when he moaned.

[19]

The owner followed the loony's eyes, and finally he took the thin sweaty dime out of his uncurled hand.

The loony hoisted up his overalls strap and went toward the tent. The owner looked after him, still wary: he'd had trouble with too many loonies after they got into the show. "How long's he been that way?" he said.

The man next in line looked at his wife. "Reckon 'bout forty years?" he said.

"Reckon so," she said. "Long's however old he is."

The man turned back. "Reckon 'bout forty years," he said.

The owner tore off two tickets, took the man's forty cents. "Think he's liable to cause any trouble?" he asked cautiously.

The man turned to his wife. "Don't reckon so, do you?" he said.

"No," she said," still standing where she was. "Might just moan a little."

"Naw, might jist moan a little," said the man, going on toward the tent, his wife going along behind.

When he had filled all the campstools in the tent, lined the kids up around the sides, the owner told the rest to come back tomorrow night and went inside. Christ, it was stuffy and smelled. He walked along the little aisle left in the sawdust, feeling their eyes in the dark watching him expectantly. When he got to the small white screen set up in front, he turned. "Joe, a light," he said.

The projection man at the back of the tent threw the spotlight on him, and a chorus of ohs rose from the crowd. The light came from behind a piece of cardboard with holes covered over by red and green and blue cellophane, so that it played across the owner's face like a rainbow. "Ain't that the berries," he said, smiling out.

He could see only those sitting along the aisle where the

light came; he noted where the loony sat — second aisle seat on the right. "Now don't worry," the owner said. "I'm not going to make a speech." He paused and everybody laughed. "I just want to tell you how glad I am to be back here," he went on, still smiling. "All the places I go, I tell that the finest folks I ever met are in Marigold, Mississippi, and from one summer till the next I look toward getting back here. So I just had to say these few words. Thank you all for coming, and I hope you like the show. Let 'er go, Joe," he said, and went to sit down.

But the light didn't go off, it just kept on playing where his face had been, only now against the white, silent screen. Everybody waited. "Joe," the owner said, wiping his forehead.

Finally somebody in the rear said, "He's outside smoking."

"Well, couldn't you tell him to come in?" the owner said.

"Reckon so," the voice said. The tent flap was lifted, and everybody looked at the thin blue line of twilight showing, commented on how no air came in. "The man says for you to come on in and get the picture started."

A red glow showed against the blue, then Joe flipped away his cigarette and closed the flap. He cut off the spotlight, started the little black box whirring, and threw the movie beam where the spotlight beam had been. Only, he threw it too high. Black-and-white words slid across the tent top upside down, while thin jumpy music began to play. Everybody sat quietly; no one would laugh, except the owner himself. He jumped up from his seat toward the side, where he could keep an eye on things, laughing nervously. "Just a minute, folks, everything'll get straightened out," he said, waving them back down as if someone had thought of leaving. It was quiet while the projection man clicked off the whirring, then started it again. The light beam came like sun dust down the aisle, and the title and the thin music came from the screen this time. There was a rustle while everybody got settled (no one would move much after the picture started) and a steady drone of voices, reading off what the titles said to those who didn't know.

The owner went back and sat down. He leaned back into the dark and had himself a good quiet laugh. "Oh, my God," he said to himself when he had finished and had taken out his handkerchief and was wiping his forehead. He'd seen the loony leaning way down off his campstool, almost on his head, watching the movie on the tent top.

Jake straightened up when the writing disappeared. He didn't know where it or the music had gone. No one else moved, so he sat quietly and folded his hands. He remembered the man who didn't want to take his dime, and saw him looking at him and laughing. So he grinned back. But the man's face went back into the dark. Then he heard the sound again, a whirring as a snake made when he tried to pick it up, and he looked for it on the tent top.

"There," the thin little girl next to him whispered, and she put her hand on his face and pulled it down, pointed it frontward.

The unexpected touch of the hand coming out of the dark sent him bolt upright. He stared straight ahead at the words, without seeing them. Then he sat back, let himself feel again how the hand had felt: soft.

Softness he understood.

The dark, the movie, the people around were lost to him now while he was remembering softness. One thing at a time he could know.

Some things he had learned: repeated things. And some

things he knew instinctively, animal-like: tones, touches, whether they were kind, or not.

The child's hand had touched him as his mother's did whenever he put his head in her lap and she held his face close. It touched him as his mother's had done when she gave him the dime.

He always wanted to hold hands when they touched him this way. But his mother had pulled back. "Now don't," she had said. "Now don't." When he tried to put his arm around her then, she had run, saying brokenly, "Oh, God, don't let him want to do that. Maybe you oughtn't to go. Naw, naw, you can go, don't cry." She had followed him as far as the gate. "But don't touch nobody, Jake. Don't *touch* nobody," she said all the time he was going down the road, as she had said so many times before.

Remembering, because it hadn't been too long, Jake did not try to find the hand in the dark now.

The movie music had begun softly at first, but now it came loud and thin, came to him slowly; then he began to listen, and there was nothing else. It came to him beautiful and sourceless and birdlike, filled the tent, and he heard it not with his ears, but way inside him. In the pit of his stomach he heard it and tasted with it his supper, the sour, warm taste of corn bread and buttermilk.

Then, as always when something moved him, the music began to creep up inside him, and he tightened his legs together. "Jake," his mother had said before he left, "if you got to go, go outside behind a tree. Please, God, let him."

He held himself rigid on the narrow campstool and continued to listen.

The music was in his chest now, hurting. It would move on up to his mouth, then it would be soundless — he knew.

He knew he had to catch it before it was soundless. He waited in the dark for the right moment, while the music sang to him as the birds do before they fly away.

"Caw, caw," the little boys would cry when Jake reached up after the birds. "I'm a bird, Jake. Catch *me*."

The music rose, and it seemed to Jake soaring, going away. This was the moment, and he began to run after it, and it seemed so close he thought this time he had caught it. Then something held him and he turned, looked into the face he had seen before with colors on it, and the owner dragged him, pushed him into his seat roughly. "Stay down, Jake," everyone called.

He felt water running down his leg, but he sat still. The music had ceased, and he had forgotten it. He simply found himself, without surprise, sitting in the dark, as often he seemed to wake from a long sleep and find himself places, and he felt if he sat quietly long enough, it would come to him why he was there. But the small voice next to him soon whispered in his ear, "Look at the pictures."

Then Jake became aware of the picture before him, and he looked at it, began to fit things together piecemeal: two men were on the white sheet; they were on horses; they held guns and pointed them in the air toward hills; one took off a big wide hat, put it on again; they tied something over their faces. The men began to talk and Jake watched the movements of their mouths beneath the masks; he could tell then their mouths were opening and closing. He listened carefully, bent forward on his stool to hear them better.

He heard what they said, heard each one. One said something and he heard him distinctly; then the other said something and he heard him, but then he could not remember what the first had said. He started over again. He leaned forward more, watched and listened carefully to each man;

would begin to think what one had said when the other would speak — and he turned his head quickly and began to think what *he* was saying. There was not enough time, and he began to feel the tightness coming on again.

People, sometimes even his mother, always spoke to him too fast. They said a word and he began to think about it, but when they continued to say words, it all became a jumble. He tried again and again to go back to the first word, but too many others had come between, and even his first faint glimmer would be gone. If there was time, he felt he could know what was said; he was sure. Often he felt that if only he had time, he could even answer.

For he felt words inside him the way he felt music. The words came to him, starting in his stomach, and he listened to them carefully while they moved on up to his chest, began to hurt him; then in a rush the words would be in his mouth, and he would open it. He would hear the words clearly, and he would smile proudly; but he knew he had not when they looked away and said, "Wipe off your mouth, Jake."

On the screen the two men went riding away suddenly toward the hills; the music came again very loud. Jake jerked up to listen, but it was not the bird music. This music went *pound pound pound*, faster and faster. It went galloping loud. It rose out of the dark and sounded terribly in his head. It went *thumpty thumpty thump*, louder and faster, came closer and closer, and he felt it was coming after him; there was no time to run from the tent. He screwed his eyes shut and pulled his head into his shoulders, held his hands over his ears hard. He ran within himself now, as he did when the little boys chased him, beating tin pails with rocks.

"I'm a bird, Jake. Listen to the birdies," the little boys would yell, running after him, beating horribly. And he would run crazily for miles, holding his ears, and long after he outran them he still heard the poundings, and not until he came to a place that was quiet and had sat for a long time could he take down his hands; then he would cry, rubbing his ears. Now he began to cry. "Shut up that noise, Jake," several of the men called out behind him in the dark.

One of the ladies leaned toward the owner. "He always tries to sing when he hears music," she explained. The movie man nodded condescendingly.

Jake stopped crying when the men yelled at him. He understood the tones of their voices. The music quieted, faded, but he sat bent over on his campstool with his head down, his hands still holding his ears.

The men spoke to him in the same tones whenever he saw them in town, leaning back in straight-legged chairs against the storefronts, hounds sleeping in circles at their feet. He had long wanted a dog; he would stop to ask the men where he could get one. As he leaned over to pat the soft warm bellies of their hounds, he would begin to tell them how he wanted a dog too. Banging their chair legs to the porch, they would jump up and yell, "Get on away, Jake. Get him away from *my* bitch. Get on, stop that there moanin'."

Then he would take himself away, telling them he would come back tomorrow to find out where he could get him a dog.

"Wake up, Jake." Behind him, a man caught hold of Jake's overalls, jerked him up. His eyes opened, astonished. He saw the tent over his head, felt the people around him in the dark, was aware of a mosquito; he remembered something had jerked him, a voice had said something. He listened to the breathing around him.

Amid the light coming down the aisle he saw faces, all looking straight ahead. He looked ahead too. He saw the picture, remembered he had seen it up front before, and re-

alized mutely that this was why he was there, to look at the
picture. He looked at it intently.

But he felt tired, as if he had been running for a long time;
he couldn't think what the picture was — it was only black-
and-white shadows. His mouth fell open and he stared straight
ahead of himself.

The thin childish voice next to him began to whisper in his
ear quietly, slowly, "They're the badmen."

Jake nodded his head slowly with each word, shook it at
the last.

His mother had primed him. She sat him down for a long
time before he came and told him what he would see; having
been to the movie three summers ago, she knew. "You'll like
the cows, the horses, the hills," she said, and made him nod
his head. "But not the badmen." Then she made him shake
it. His mother never let him talk, though he wanted to. "You
don't have to talk, son," she would say. "You don't have to.
Be quiet now."

It was hotter than ever in the tent now, as if twenty-five
people sitting still for an hour had breathed up all the air.
Next to the child a woman began to fan herself, and when
she leaned around and fanned the child too, Jake felt a small
breeze; he let himself feel it and smell the smell that came
with it, sweet, the way his mother smelled when she put
powder on her face.

The woman looked away and he followed her gaze. He saw
a man riding a horse, coming slowly down a road. Everyone
in the crowd began to clap; the little boys in the back whistled.
Jake smiled, then he laughed, cupped his big pawlike hands
together and pulled them apart, made a slapping sound like
everyone else. He watched his hands going together, coming
apart, making a noise; then the little-girl voice whispered,
"Quit now," and he quit.

[27]

He looked where the little girl looked, watched the man on the horse again. The man opened his mouth and began to sing. Jake rocked back and forth on his campstool as the man rocked back and forth on his horse, and he heard the singing inside him and smiled to himself. He had known for a long time that he could sing. Whenever he was alone he would sing, but he kept it a secret.

The man sang loudly and Jake grinned wider now, knowing the sounds in him to be the same as the man made. When the child next to him, lost in the movie, leaned against his shoulder, he turned and looked at her face, small, perspiring, openmouthed; he saw her breath going in time to the music, and he remembered her voice touching his ear, her hand touching his face a long time ago, and it came to him suddenly to tell her he could sing. Softly, with closed eyes, he began to sing, wanting just this one small face to know his secret. Abruptly the face hissed close to his, snakelike, "Shhh, you shut up that moanin'," and he felt a breeze beat in his face very hard. He opened his eyes and looked into an angry face with a tongue shooting out like the snake's did, with eyes that were two hard slits. The woman had jerked the little girl away, was there in her place.

Jake turned away frightened, hunched up on his stool, keeping himself away, his song forgotten. Was he supposed to run? He did not know. He sat on in the dark, trembling until his back began to ache so he had to move. Cautiously he slid his feet from under the stool, gradually straightened his cramped legs; the face didn't turn on him. Stealthily then he eased out his back, sat up. Over the head in front of him he saw the movie again.

A man got off a horse, went up to a girl, stroked her long hair, talking softly. Jake's eyes followed the stroking up and down, and slowly his fingers began to curl, uncurl, against the rough knee of his overalls.

"Shh, shh," the snake face said. Jake jumped, but the face was not looking at him; it was turned toward the back where the little boys hooted like owls.

He watched the stroking again — soft, soft, he knew, remembering Sarah Jane. He began to ache, remembering Sarah Jane.

"Sarah Jane, Sarah Jane," he would moan softly over and over, stroking her. And she never moved, she never pulled away from him. She just listened to him. When he had finished all he had to say, she would look at him with unwavering eyes. Spent with telling at last, he would sit down then and, leaning his head into her stomach, begin to milk her. When the sweet, warm milk came, he would sometimes begin to cry, because of the stillness and the listening that was Sarah Jane; he would tell her then how she was the only one who would listen. But soon his mother would come running down to the cowshed, screaming, "Get away from her now, Jake. Get away!" And she would take him away. All the time going to the house he tried to tell her about Sarah Jane, but she would say, "Hush now, hush." Then he would cry, looking back at Sarah Jane watching him with her calm brown eyes.

When the man stopped stroking, Jake's fingers hesitated, half curled. He sat waiting, but the screen flickered, the scene changed, and the man was gone. There were horses instead, pounding frightfully going over a hill, and the sound of gunshots. Not only the next face but all the faces hissed, and twenty-five pairs of feet thudded dully against the sawdust. Jake laughed, picked up one of his feet, then the other, set each down in the sawdust, stomping too.

Suddenly, through a cloud of dust on the screen, he saw

a cow face come toward him with wild frightened eyes, mooing loudly and mournfully. He stood up. "Sara Jane, Sarah Jane," he called again and again, beginning to run. The owner grabbed him by his crossed straps and one sleeve, dragged him down the light beam through the aisle of snickering faces, and out into the night. "God damn you, loon," he muttered.

Jake pulled back toward the tent, but the man shook him hard; then Jake forgot about the tent. He stood bewildered, with the man's face breathing close to his. "You're not getting back in there," the owner gritted out between his teeth.

With no thought left of what was inside the tent, Jake stood limply while the owner held him. Finally the owner released him and lit a cigarette, stood facing him, waiting to overcome his anger. "Just God damn you," he said as he drew on the cigarette, which glowed faintly red against his face in the dark.

And this faint red glow stirred up, as much as possible, a memory in Jake. When he had seen the owner with the spotlight playing across his face, he had associated it with the one thing of color indelibly etched on his mind — the sunset — because he watched it daily, and now he knew that he had seen this face before with color on it. He began to tell the man. "Take your hands off me. Get on away," the owner said, giving him a good shove before he threw away his cigarette and went on back into the tent.

Jake turned after him, knew from the tone of the voice not to follow, and stood holding on to the outside fold of the tent flap, beginning to tell the man about the sun going down red against a darkening sky. In a little while someone stuck his head out. "Shut up that noise and go home," he said, and while the tent flap was open Jake glimpsed a man and a girl, heard music, saw a horse with its mane waving in the wind; then he was staring at nothing, with his nose up against the closed flap of the tent.

He turned, ran his hand over his nose where the rough tent had scratched it, and went on slowly down the faint road. The moon came out smiling from behind a cloud, opened up a white path; he followed it, listening to the staccato sounds from katydids hiding in the tall grass alongside the road, listening to the shrill loud screaming of locusts from somewhere overhead, listening to the stumbling crunch of his own feet on the gravel, all sounds.

Alone, he began to call up words from way inside him. A bird fluttered in one of the poplar trees, and he looked for it between the white leaves. It sang sleepily way up, and he went on. He went instinctively, not having to think where he was going. Because it was quiet the words came easily but formed slowly, one by one, and he waited for them to come as he walked.

When he had been in the quiet for about a mile, he began to remember: music. He stored up words to go with the music. After a while he remembered the horse, and he stored up words to go with the horse. He remembered the wind.

He turned out of the moonlight and went through the dark again, his feet following surely the thin side road.

When he saw the little house, with one lighted window, he went up to it and looked inside. A woman knelt by a bed, and he watched her. As she stood up and got into bed, he saw without surprise that it was his mother and knew he was home. His mother sat in the bed by the lamp and he knew she was waiting for him. He waited, watching her. The night sounds continued around him; they had become part of his hearing now, and he did not have to listen to them consciously. With the sounds around him, with the words inside him, he felt again the uncontrollable thing that guided him, and he wanted to make sounds too. He moved his hands out in a sweeping gesture, stood out-

side the window, nodded his head up and down, shook it once.
But the words still stirred him, wanting to be said. Suddenly
he found himself going away from the window, and he went,
went as if he were following himself.

He went quietly through the tall, dew-wet grass, felt it itch
his leg, but he forgot it before he could remember to stop and
scratch. He went on with the words carefully inside him. The
music began, churned inside him with the words, words about
the horse with its mane waving in the wind, and he held
everything inside him together as much as he could, till the
moment to tell them.

He found himself at the gate, lifted it and set it back into
its rut. Then he went silently, smelling the ragweed, heard
frog music, and he heard it and set it apart slowly from his
own music. Instinctively he went on through the dark and
circled wide around the place where he had seen the snake.

As he went down into the summer-dried ditch, came up
again, the words jarred loose from his chest and he started
running, telling them.

As he heard the first faint bell tinkle, he was running faster,
telling about the wind, waving his arms.

He smelled the pasture for the first time as he came up to
her, and he lay down immediately with his head on her soft
flank. When he felt her stillness and her warm breath smelling
of grass, he began to tell her about the music, and he knew,
as much as he could, that through the long summer he would
come here again and again.

The Sound of Silence

*S*HE was dead. He knew it was death. She did not move for a very long time while he watched, and then he knew it was death. He had loved animals and they had been taken from him, but only after he had watched a long time and they had stayed still. And she was that still, like everywhere after a summer storm. He sat, and in the way that was his, after a time he said, "Ma . . ."

She did not answer. She had not answered him all morning. When he opened his eyes to daytime, for the first time in the forty years of his life he had not heard her in the house. He knew it was home. The window was by the bed, and above his head was where the rain had come and spread long brown streaks that dried and peeled.

He got out of bed and went along the long hall, his feet cool on the bare floor, until he came to the room that was hers. He sat down watching; then it was two days, and he was tired. He got up, thinking how the cat ate mice that died and the dog went under the house with snakes; a cow down by the pond had stayed until there was nothing left but bones the buzzards had left.

He went outdoors, aware of the long, hot grass reaching after his legs as he crossed the yard. The chickens ran at him angrily, flew up at his knees and pecked the rounded toes of his worn-out brogans. He looked up at the sun, went inside the feedhouse and after a while came out with the right gunnysack. He stood, a tall thin figure against the sunlight, still except for the swinging arc of his arm spreading the feed about him. When it was done, he put the sack back exactly right and went on down to the back of the yard. He picked up a chick that came running in a great fright from inside the little shed when he opened the door. He held its soft yellow roundness close to him, sitting on the hole that pinched his bottom. And he tried to tell the animal in great dry sobs, but he knew no words for loss.

Finally he was crying for her. He came out blowing his nose on his sleeve and he set the chick down; still stooping, he watched as it ran toward the feed, crazylike, on its little thin legs. Then going on, he began to remember what she had always told him, and he fastened his overalls. He hesitated at the steps leading up to the porch and looked at the house. It seemed dark inside after the brightness behind him, and he sat down on the steps and began to pull at the long summer-smelling grass crowding around him. The blades were slick and green and broke open wetly as his fingernail pressed into them. He sat a long time pulling the blades one by one, pressing them open, and then laying them neatly in a pile alongside him. Squirrels stole pecans from the heavy greenness of the tree just beyond the gate, and at that instant a thin brown-and-white hound appeared in the empty road from the depths of the orchard and trotted in sidelong fashion toward the gate; working it open with his nose, the dog came into the yard, sniffing. Having nosed the pile of grass blades, the hound sat back on its haunches watching, hot and dusty, with red tongue lolling sideways out of a space between its teeth.

Presently Jake rose and walked out again into the yard from which he had just come, his eyes fixed where they had been for some time, as if to move them would be to forget. He walked to where the two-days-hung sheets idled stiffly in the one breath of air that stirred. He fumbled about them for some time, but finally his fingers found their answer and he began to pull the sheets gently from the line. Crumpling them between his two great hands, he carried them carefully toward the house and gained the porch and was entering the house itself when its silence stopped him. He offered the sheets and withdrew them; offered them again anyway while the enormous tears that were his kind came down his cheeks. Behind him the hound, which had not yet moved, rose at the sound that spoke to it and, ambling to the man's heels, sat again on its haunches and, lifting its head, began a similar sound.

Then Jake turned for the first time, seeming to notice the dog, and looking down at it, was silent. The dog hushed too; it looked up eagerly, its drooling mouth open again. And then he heard the rumblings of his own stomach.

He stood a long time not knowing what to do. In his whole life he had never fixed food. Shortly, as if led by something unseen, he went the length of the house and entered the kitchen, with the dog just after him.

Someone had been there recently. Two places were laid opposite each other on the small oilcloth-covered table. The cover to a jar of grape jelly had slipped askew and black ants filled the jar's empty half. He smelled oilcloth and crackers stored against wetness in an old wooden cabinet propped against the far wall. He went to it and opened the doors; then the smell of confined bread was even stronger. He saw cold biscuits and wedges of corn bread on a chipped white plate, and he took the plate down, already crowding food into his mouth. The dog whined and he threw it a biscuit; the dog gulped it whole, then twitched its behind, whining again. He threw it the last of the corn bread and watched as the dog wolfed it, scattering crumbs in all directions. He stood, waiting, listening; in the silence, he heard a fly buzz. Presently something led him to the other side of the house, to the screened porch. He lowered a bucket into the cistern and brought up water and they both drank from the dipper.

Sometime in the late afternoon, after he had gone many times into her room and looked at her and come out again and walked around the house and returned again and repeated the whole process, he found himself going down the road on his way to town. At each bend in the road he turned back, his face screwed up as he faced the sun's setting, his arm raised and gesturing, his throat convulsive, and the empty countryside filled with all the sounds he could utter: telling her he was going for help. Then, going on, he stopped again, each time uttering the sounds again, but sometimes gently, and with a meaning so different the sounds themselves sounded different; stooping, holding out his hand, trying to snap his fingers, calling the dog that had fled with a great yelp after the first time it had entered her room with him and sniffed around the bed.

The sun had gone by the time he entered town, but there were several hours of daylight left yet. The sun's passing made the day a little cooler and the shirt stuck wetly to his back began to dry as he gained the wooden sidewalks of the town and with a high loping step picked his way between the broken planks.

"Here he comes," called someone from the porch of the first store.

"Where you been, Jake?" called somebody else sitting in the circle of cane-bottomed chairs.

[38]

As he came up to the little store, another man said, "You been up to Memphis going to town, Jake?" and everybody laughed.

The first man shot a long brown stream of tobacco over his stomach and into the grass. "Naw," he said, "I bet he's been up to Washington, D.C., helping out there, hey, Jake?" and everybody laughed so hard Cotter May had a terrible fit of coughing.

The mute stood shaking his head, saying the sound that was *n*.

"He says naw," somebody said, and somebody else said, "Well, where you been at, Jake?"

He hung his head and went on. Somebody called after him, "You ain't crazy, are you, Jake?" and somebody else called the answer, "Naw, but you ain't far from it are you, Jake?" And this time the laughter was drowned out by the sound of flying gravel as a car from the country tore through town too fast.

He was alone until he crossed the side road and came to the next store. Nothing but a hound was on the porch. He tried to step over it, but miscalculated distance as he often did and stepped on its tail. He felt a great rush of pity, but at the dog's yowling someone opened the screen door into him and he forgot the dog.

"Oh, it's just a houn'," the woman said, and stepped aside. "How you, Jake?" she said as he came in; then, shifting a large sack of groceries, she started for the door; but he brushed at her arm, afraid to touch it, remembering not to touch anyone; tears came with his effort and when he opened his mouth, nothing came out except saliva.

"Oooo, I declare to my soul," the woman said, turning away. She was quite large, going down the walk in a dress patterned all over with large purple poppies. He felt dizzy watching the design in motion as she walked away. Someone spoke to him from behind the counter, a face kind and familiar. "Jake, do you want to go to the bathroom? It's right back there through that door." He stood just inside the store shaking his head, trying to seek control over crying. The tears welled in his eyes as he stood blinking; finally they welled over.

"You take him, Thomas," the woman said. A little Negro boy seated on a pile of feed sacks stared at her openmouthed and said, "Naw sir, Miss Loma, he liable to have warts."

"Oh, get on out of here," she said, and the little boy picked up a bottle of orange pop and fled. Taking Jake's elbow, she propelled him to his duty. He performed it. When he returned, she scanned to see that he had closed his fly.

"You wanna banana caramel, Jake?" she said, reaching into the mottled case. He shook his head. Her hand moved from one box of candy to another, touching them lightly. "Candy ice-cream cone? Sour ball? Baseball sucker? Not licorice," she said, turning up her nose. He shook his head each time. "Sure you do," she said, and her hand returned to the caramels, deciding for him. She took one of the hard yellow squares from the case and put it into his hand. He stood looking down at it. "Here," she said, and took it and removed the slick waxed paper. Then she put it into his hand again, and as soon as he smelled its sweetness, saliva formed in his mouth and he felt hunger pains in his stomach. He put it into his mouth.

Two men stopped a small tractor outside the door and came inside with a heavy clumping of boots and a terrible smell of sweat. They took Cokes out of the ice case and settled into chairs. Miss Loma leaned over the counter and talked to them, stopping several times for children who came for Popsicles, or for ladies who had forgotten several little things when they shopped in the morning, or who just wanted a cold Coke.

Jake stood at his spot. If someone spoke to him, he rolled his eyes in their direction. The candy was a large unmelting hump in his cheek. Once a little boy howled, "You got mumps, Jake!" and the little girl with him ran screaming into the road.

"If he weren't Brother Patrick's boy, I declare to my soul, I don't know what all I wouldn't do to that child," Miss Loma said, and shook her head. She picked up the empty bottles the men had left and put them into the Coke case. "Where's your ma, Jake?" she said. "She didn't shop Monday."

His eyes and mouth opened in a round surprised manner, the candy fell from inside his cheek into the center of his mouth, and his teeth fell shut over it. Suddenly the sweetness began to flow down his throat, and pressed against the roof of his mouth, the caramel began to melt — it was suddenly soft-feeling, and he touched it experimentally with his tongue.

"Good?" Miss Loma said. "Want another?" But she was busy straightening up the counter at that moment and did not get it.

He knew that there was something besides the candy; a thought had been just within reach and now hung just out of it. As best he could, he searched for it. But he could not push aside the taste, the smell, the feel of the candy, and he could know fully only one thing at a time. Miss Loma was leading him to the door now, telling him it was time for him to go home, time to close the store. He suddenly stood on the porch and watched the door closed in his face. The candy was still too large for him to speak. Miss Loma stood inside motioning him down the road, her face a round white circle against the dark interior.

He turned finally. A few pink tinges remained in the sky,

but for the most part it was rain-gray. He walked in the twilight through the almost empty town. Miss Alma, the postmistress, was rocking on her front porch and said, "Evenin', Jake." Behind her, her lamp was a warm yellow spot in the growing dark. Crickets in the deep grass along the roadside began to sound. Ahead, a man was pumping water for his horse in a little shed set in the center of town; the clang of the iron pump was loud in the supper-hour quiet, as was even the rush of water and the sound of the horse's drinking. "Evenin', Jake," the man said and doffed his hat. "How's your ma?" And he turned back to the horse, expecting no answer. He did not even see Jake stop and stand and look. He got on his horse and rode away in the opposite direction, leaving behind a cloud of dust that filtered through Jake's nostrils, seeped even through his lips closed tightly over the candy, flavoring it with dust and grit, and hurting his eyes, until the postmistress called gently through the near-dark, "Get out of the dust, Jake."

Then he moved, his gaunt figure continuing in its funny high loping step down the middle of the road. He turned off the main road and down a side one that he would follow to its very end. He passed all the houses and went for some time along the road, which narrowed until it was hardly big enough for one car; on each side was a shallow ditch, weed-filled, and beyond them nothing but gullies and pastureland; occasionally he smelled wild plum and honeysuckle and once the tickling, pepperish smell of tiny wild roses; but mostly he smelled the stink of ragweed and simply the heavy grassy smell of summer.

His shoes hurt him and a rock had bruised an instep through one thin sole. He was feeling the pain of it when suddenly he gave a little choking sound and with a last flood of sweetness the candy slipped down the back of his throat, leaving his mouth, at last, free. For a while he could think only of that and went over and over the surprise of losing the candy. But then he suddenly sat down on the side of the road and, with his head hung between his knees, moaned over and over all that he had wanted to say. Spent at last, he got up and continued on the road until he came up against the gate.

He stood outside and looked at the dark house. It was the first time in his life there had been no one to meet him and no lamp lit. When he had passed through the gate, he went forward hesitantly, his mouth hung open, his hands groping toward the side of the house, though dark had not yet come full. He entered, closing the door softly behind him, and stared down the long dark hall, expecting still that someone would come into it. He went its length and reached the kitchen and saw it the same as he had quit it a long time ago. He went into all the rooms of the house, hers among them, and looked at her without surprise, and continued to look about the house, still expecting someone. At last he did not know what to do with himself, though he knew the ritual that should be followed. He went finally and got into bed, all her warnings clear in his head. He looked once toward the lamp, but he did not touch it.

The next morning he found milk and bread and butter. He went out across the yard to the henhouse and carried in eggs in a worn enamel pan, but once inside, he put them in the center of the table, not knowing what else to do with them. He was sitting at the kitchen table, still in the clothes he had slept in, very carefully using a knife to put butter on his bread, when he heard a truck come to a stop. He put all the bread into his mouth and sat very quietly, chewing. He heard the car door slam, and presently he heard the scrape of the screen door being pulled open across the floor; then he heard heavy footsteps. He was hidden by the door when someone came into the room next to him — the dining room, where the icebox was kept. He could see slightly between the doorframe and the door as the big colored man struggled to lift the fifty pounds of ice into the box. Then he slung the tongs over his shoulder and called, "Missus, it's Preacher with the ice."

In the silence afterward, Jake could hear the man's heavy breathing. He knew who the man was and why he was there. He knew that now it was going to be all right. Soon the man moved to the door of the bedroom and called, "Hello, Missus."

Jake could hear the alarm clock ticking in there. Then he could hear the heavy steps of the man going away, and his voice, fainter, calling, "It's Preacher."

Then the man was on the front porch. Jake heard the door slam behind him. And he knew how it would look: the empty porch, the stilled swing, ahead the empty road and quiet flatland; and the field, still too, rising in the distance to a road where you could see the white steeple of the church. He thought he heard a bird sing, and he could feel the warmth of the day flush on his face as he knew the man could; sweat stood out on his forehead.

Presently he heard the man open the front door to reenter the house, and he stood up and went down the hall, meaning neither to be quiet nor to make noise, but the man did not hear him. He was in her room, bending over the bed. Jake stood outside the door, watching. He heard the man's heavy intake of breath, watched as he drew the sheet up over her face. The man came into the hall and followed it to the kitchen.

Jake was seated again at the table, a piece of bread halfway to his mouth. He looked up at the man without sound or expression, and the man gazed back at him silently. Once he opened his mouth as if to say something, but then he closed it and his head gave a little shake. He leaned against the doorframe and wiped his face with a handkerchief; then he sort of half blew his nose and shook his head again and went on out the back door. Jake heard the flutter and squawking of chickens and heard the man spreading their feed. For a while he heard nothing, then the man's voice farther away calling, "Su pig pig pig," and the sound of corncobs falling into their trough. In a little while he came back up the short hill, puffing from the climb, and passed the back door and said, "No time now for a cow." He stood at the bottom of the back steps and called up, "You stay there. You stay there. You hear, Mister Jake?"

Jake buttered a slice of bread and put it into his mouth. It was then, while he was chewing, he knew that sometime before he had heard the truck drive away. He got up and went down the hall and took the sheet away from her face. Then he returned to his seat in the kitchen.

When the first ones to hear the news came, he was still sitting there: still eating the loaf of bread and the hand-shaped mound of white butter.

"You eat that whole loaf, Jake?" said one of the ladies.

When he looked up, there was a whole brood of them looking at him from a semicircle; their brightness almost frightened him. They wore flowered dresses and colored glass beads; their cheeks were red spots and their mouths narrow red lines; their faces were freshly powdered, and some were the color of flour while others were like peaches in bloom. One lady, with bracelets that slid down her arm when she reached out, took the bread away from him, though he was still hungry.

"Oh, the poor *thing*," said another. "Do you think he knows?"

"Bound to," said another. "He's bound to've looked into her room. They say it's been several days."

"But I mean, do you think he *understands*?" said the other.

[45]

They were all silent, looking at him. Finally one said, "Come on out on the porch, Jake, and get some fresh air."

He got up and followed her. The others came behind. "We could take his mind off it," said one, "if only we knew whether it was *on* it or not." She looked back at the near-empty polka-dotted bread wrapper.

Miss Hattie McGaha, a thin little birdlike lady, said, "Well, there's no sense fixing him something to eat," and she followed the others, fluttering her hands helplessly.

From the porch he could see others coming, clouds of dust preceding and following the various cars, horses, trucks; some came on foot at a half-run, shielding their faces as vehicles passed them and arriving covered with a gold-colored film. They came through the gate, subdued, and greeted one another on the porch in quiet tones. Jake sat in a rocking chair in the midst of them, staring out at the front yard. Everyone looked at him but no one spoke except two or three men in shirtsleeves who patted him on the back and said, "It's okay, boy. It's okay."

The ladies stood off together in a little cluster, just not knowing this time what to do at all.

Whenever there had been a death, he had gone too; now one had come home to him. People were coming here. Brother Patrick came, wearing a suit even though it was summertime. People stepped aside as he came up and shook Jake's hand, the way he would have done with anyone. Then he opened his mouth as if he wanted to say something, but nothing seemed to come, so he closed it and just shook harder. Someone whispered into his ear, "She's inside, Brother Patrick." Then he let go of Jake's hand and went into the house.

Things moved on through the afternoon like that. People were all over the porch and the yard, in groups now, talking louder, laughing if they wanted. Once someone brought him

[46]

a glass of iced tea, and once someone brought him a bowl of homemade ice cream. It was then a long car came down the road and pulled around to the side of the house. By the time he finished the ice cream, it had gone slowly away, and a man near him remarked that it was a relief to get that done. Someone touched him on the shoulder to go to the bathroom, and when he passed through the kitchen he saw more cakes and pies on the table than he had ever seen all together before. He sat on the porch again later, thinking of them. The sound of talking went on around and above him, rising and falling like bee hums; he rocked with the rhythm, warm air falling over him and falling away again, the smells of grass and clover so intense he knew how it would feel to have his face in them.

For a while all he knew after that was the far-off hum of speech and the sweet smell of clover; and after that, for a long time, all he knew was the look of the black car going away.

When he woke, he saw a group of people standing at the gate, shaking hands all around. Carrying cakes and pies, everyone left but two men. The one he knew best, Wilroy Sheaffer, said, "He's awake," as they came back across the porch.

The other, Cotter May, said, "You want some supper, Jake?"

There were still a few people in the yard, and he could hear someone in the house. The day had lessened, and with it the heat. He stretched his legs out and rocked a little bit, and then he nodded. Just as the two men were turning away, Jake got up suddenly and caught Wilroy by the sleeve. He told him and told him about the chickens, pointing at the henhouse until finally Wilroy understood. "You hear that, Cotter?" he said. "He knows it's time to feed them chickens. It's been done, Jake," he said. "It's all done been taken care of. Everything." Wilroy called into the kitchen to his wife, who had been a friend of Jake's mother. "Mary Margaret! Woman, fix this boy some supper."

When his wife came from the kitchen, he said, "Do you know this boy knew it was time to feed them chickens?"

Mary Margaret beamed at Jake. "Well, now, I declare. Your supper's on the table, Jake. *Table*," she said, raising her voice and her finger to point at the same time.

Everybody watched him as he went inside. "That *boy* is near 'bout old as I am," Cotter said from the swing.

"Oh well, you know," Mary Margaret said, in a hushing tone.

Cotter's spinster sister, Ruth Edna, who had been closer to Jake and his mother than anyone, had come onto the porch from the kitchen now. She gave Cotter a swat on the head with one of the cardboard fans the undertaker had left. "Now we don't know how much *he does know*," she said.

Mary Margaret said, "We ought to go inside and see about him. We're the ones to, now."

"Well, then we got to get on home," Wilroy said.

They all went down the hall, single file. "I hate to think of all we got to do when we get there," Mary Margaret said.

The Mays lived together, and Ruth Edna looked over her shoulder at her brother. "Us too," she said meaningfully.

"Now I don't no'm," Cotter said, grimacing. He rubbed his hand across his back. "This day has been about all I can take. I'm wore out." He coughed lightly, ignoring the thin set of his sister's lips.

Jake was seated at the table carefully picking the lima beans out of his bowl of succotash — popping them into his mouth and sucking his fingers loudly. They all huddled around him making little sounds, offering a spoon and tucking a napkin under his chin. Finally they decided to leave him alone. "Let be what'll be," was the way Wilroy put it; and they were all anxious to get home.

The last stragglers, who had been on a little inspection tour of the house and yard, came around to the back of the house just then and yelled up that they were going. "Wait a minute," Mary Margaret said. "Did you all bring the chocolate cake or the banana pudding?"

"Pudding and a little pan of fudge," came back the answer. "Eloise says leave that."

Mary Margaret carried the food out onto the porch. "No sense leaving them here for him to get sick on eating them all up at once."

She came back into the house and when her somewhat broad expanse had cleared the doorway, Jake saw the two containers being carried away as the others had been. The little tin pan of fudge caught a last glint of afternoon sun and shone for a second like silver. The succotash was tasteless in his mouth tuned for sweetness. The two women, who had looked around their dead friend's house to see that everything was all right, came back now, bustling themselves together, ready to go. "Well, boy," Wilroy said.

"Well," Mary Margaret said.

"There's milk in the box," Ruth Edna said. "*Milk.*"

"I hate to leave him," Mary Margaret said. "Dark coming on. You think he knows how to light the lamp?"

"Sure," Wilroy said. "He knew about them chickens, didn't he? Don't forget to feed the chickens tomorrow now, boy," he said, louder. "And if you don't know what to do with that cow, put a rope around her neck and bring her into town. Somebody'll help you."

"He can't understand all that," his wife said.

"Shoot," Wilroy said, as if somebody were deaf, "that boy

can understand more'n we think he can. Come on. We got to get home, woman."

The women stood at the table, looking down at the last two cakes. Between them, Jake looked up at them and then down at the cakes. "You reckon we ought to leave one?" Mary Margaret said.

"Oh, I reckon one," Miss May said. "It seems so funny giving all those others back like that."

"Well, we couldn't have left them here for him to eat all up at once," Mary Margaret said.

"No," said the other. "And wasn't there a lot! Wouldn't she have been proud?"

"Bless her heart," Mary Margaret said. "Do you want to leave yours or mine?"

"Oh, I don't know," Ruth Edna said. They studied the two. "Mine's not much. Just something I did up as quick as I could when I heard. Fell a little. Didn't give it good time to cool."

Mary Margaret put her head on one side. "Hmm, a little," she said. "Not your best." They looked at hers: angel food with a perfect rise, and sworls of white icing lapping each other all over it; all the ladies had exclaimed. "I did put a little into mine," she said. "I tell you. I could take mine on to the cake sale at the Baptist church tomorrow."

"Well, go ahead," Ruth Edna said. "Mine's little anyway. Here, Jake. Here, honey. Eat this nice cake." She cut him a piece and put it on the side of his plate. "I'm going to put the rest up here," she said, and put the plate in the top part of the cupboard.

"He's watching," Mary Margaret said.

"Well," Miss May said, hesitantly. "Oh come on, they're blowing the horn."

Mary Margaret took her cake and followed her out of the room; then she suddenly came running back in and said,

"Bye-bye, Jake, honey. Bye-bye. You come uptown soon now, you hear."

Evening was coming. There was quiet in the chicken yard and quiet out over the garden. Beyond it, dark had come into the gullies, and a row of little wild persimmon trees stood out black on the horizon. He could see all the way across to them from where he sat in the kitchen, and two birds, black ravens against the red-and-gold sky, hovered over them an instant, then settled out of sight. In the silence of outdoors, he heard a walnut fall from the old tree in the side yard and break open against the hard ground. And in the silence of the house he heard only the clock in the bedroom and the sound of his own breathing. He was alone and he knew that.

Presently he ate the cake. His fingers dug into and out of the dark sticky chocolate, and he sucked them loudly, glad of his own noise. He had no hunger for more when he finished the piece, and did not move from the table. He could feel that beyond him the house was dark, knew that, sitting in the doorway, he was watching the last of daylight. Occasionally, from a good distance away, he would catch the sound of a car horn. He thought of the dog and wished that it had not left him. He remembered the whole afternoon and was glad of the noise and the people as they had moved about him. He wished they had not gone away.

When the kitchen had grown dark, he moved his chair out onto the old lean-to porch where there was still light enough to see a little ahead of himself. His hands hung empty and still between his knees, and he wondered if it was time for him to go to bed.

A flashlight suddenly shone on and off at the bottom of the steps like a giant mosquito. Then a voice said through the dark, "It's Jurldeane, Mister Jake." He heard her approach, and presently she was right by him and had turned the flashlight on underneath her chin. "See," she said. "Jurldeane. Your momma's wash girl."

She flashed the light around inside the kitchen. He watched it bounce ball-like from one wall to another; then it fell on the lamp. "Come on inside, Mister Jake, and let's get us some light," she said. He followed her and stood quietly while she lit the lamp. In the dark he could smell on her clothes Clorox and a clean starchy smell; when she moved he smelled her body, warm with the effort of her walk; then, with the sudden yellow light making dark hollows in her face as she bent over to turn up the wick, he smelled kerosene.

"You eat supper, I see," she said, looking down at his used dishes. He followed her glance and looked down at them too. Then when she raised her eyes, he raised his and they looked at each other across the lamplight. "I knew they wouldn't be here now," she said. Her full bottom lip, opening, was shiny with snuff. "Here you are. Here I am. Where are they?" she said. "Leaving you all alone the first night they took her away." Her mouth closed with a clamp, and she sat down heavily in the rickety kitchen chair.

"Po' thing," she said, watching his face as he sat down opposite. Suddenly she leaned out and brought his plate across the table toward her. "What's this? Choc'late cake? Whose, you reckon?" She licked her finger, then slid it across the plate where the cake had been and licked it again. "Not Miss Mary Margaret's." She considered, running her tongue all around her lips. "Don't recognize that," she said, finally. "Is they mo'?"

He followed her arm as it motioned the plate about. "Mo'?" she said.

The plate rested on the table again and she tapped it with a large forefinger. "Cake?" He looked up and met the eyes that asked him something. The head cocked to one side. "Hmmum," she said, finally. "Po' thing," and she put her hands on the table and pushed herself up. She looked behind the old curtain covering the shelves on one side of the room and then crossed over to the cupboard and opened that. She turned, grinning at him, the cake plate in her hand.

"Here it is," she said, coming back to the table. "We going to have us some cake eatin' now, Mister Jake. It going to be me and you." She pushed his plate back to him and set one down in front of herself. She cut two large pieces and placed one on each plate; then she broke off a piece of hers with her fingers and ate it. Her tongue curled around each fingertip afterward, licking them one by one. Jake watched, and when she said, "Eat that cake up," he began to eat. She smiled at him when he licked his fingers, and he opened his mouth wide showing his teeth. Once she stopped chewing and said, "Huh, oleo," and then began to chew again.

Jake finished first, and she cut him a thin sliver to eat on while she finished. He did not understand at first, and the woman said again, "Go 'head." He ate, and when they had both finished, she put slices on their plates again. She got up once and went into the next room; he sat without chewing, thinking she had gone; then she reappeared, a pitcher of milk in her hand, and poured them glasses full. They sat back in their chairs, alternately eating and licking and drinking, with no other light in the house, and no other sound save that of the clock. Her face was shining and dark in the pale light, and he did not once take his eyes from it. Whenever she looked at him, she smiled or refilled his glass or his plate. She caught a lightning bug in her hand, then released it for him to see; they watched it flicker away into the dark of the house beyond them.

"No noise. No light. Nuthin'," Jurldeane said. She was quiet a moment, listening. Jake stopped chewing, watching her. "I use' to pass by on the road upside this house some evenin's," she said. He watched as a sweat bead slid from her forehead down the side of her face, watched as she leaned over and lowered the wick of the lamp. "And we would wonder what goes on inside that house when night comes. What do he do. It always so quiet, so still like. Only sometime we see your momma passing up and down before the light, going from one room to another. Never did see you, Mister Jake. We would wonder — do he go to bed soon as dark comes, or do he set around and make some kind of talk with his momma so she have some company?" She was quiet a moment, thinking back; then she looked up at him, her eyes wide and wet. "Now I know," she said. "Now I know."

She sat back, her arms crossed beneath her breasts. "We all got some kind of cross to bear," she said. "Your momma had hers. But what I don't see, though the Lord has His ways, is who else going to take it up now."

By the light of the lamp, her eyes looked deep in their bright, white sockets. He watched them, listening to the soft singsong of her voice. And suddenly she was saying, "Oh Lord, hush now. Hush, Lamb of God."

She came around the table and pressed his head against her skirt. Once again, and for the last time, he had the warm body smell of a woman's lap for his head.

She held him until he was spent, murmuring, "Po' thing, po' old man child," and finally lifted his head and said, "Now blow your nose." And he took the paper napkin she handed him and tried to do it.

"I don't know what you going to do, Mister Jake, I declare to my soul I don't." She stood looking down into the lamp as if it might hold an answer. Then she looked at him and said, "You know how to light this thing? Turn it down and blow it out?" He looked at her eagerly, silently, mouth hung open. "You don't any more know what I'm talking 'bout than the cat flies," she said. "Here." From the curtained shelves she took a box of old candle ends, lit one and let it drip into a saucer. Then she secured the candle in the hot tallow and put it on the table before him. "You know how to blow that out?" she said. He leaned forward and did it with a little puff of spit. "Now I'm going to light it again," she said, "and when you get into bed, you be sure and blow it out, you hear? Can you nod your head if you hear?" He did that.

"I got to go now," she said. "It's on about nine o'clock." She collected the dishes from the table and rinsed them in a bucket of water sitting in the sink, then laid them on the drainboard. "Eat from these tomorrow," she said. She looked back at him, feeling that his eyes had never left her.

"I declare to my soul I don't," she said. She picked up her flashlight and tested it. His eyes blinked with the on-and-off of the light. Then she came across the room and began turning down the wick bit by bit. But suddenly she stopped when it was almost out. They were still, looking at each other, their faces shadowed with the wick's final fluttering. "I don't want to," she said, "but I got to." Then she blew out the wick, and they were alone by the thin light of the candle.

He knew that now she was going.

She stood in the doorway and looked back at him. "Get into bed now," she said. "Blow out that candle."

He made no movement, no sign. His arms lay along the table encircling the empty plate; his hands were still. Suddenly the leg bent up under his chair gave an involuntary jerk and straightened out before him with a scrape of his heel. He jumped and ran his thumb under his overall strap, pulling it back up onto his shoulder. He stared straight ahead of himself for a while. Then he put his fingers in his plate and slowly began to eat again.

"Something will happen, Mister Jake." She stood hesitantly, weighing the flashlight in her hand. "And I tell you," she said, "I will be over myself to see to yo' wash."

She looked once over her shoulder at the dark, at the direction in which she would go. The sky was lightened a moment by heat and she saw off as far as the persimmon trees. There was no sound in all of the countryside and then she heard him. The sound evoked a rush of her own tears, and she gasped to keep them back for now. She almost went, but then she took one more look at the thin, straightened legs in their dirty, creased overalls, and at the bent shoulders in the once starched shirt so carefully turned at the collar, and she came back into the room. She stood just behind him — in all instinct yearning to touch him again. But this time she did not. She bent low toward his back and whispered in a voice just before sobbing, "It ain't right. I know that. The Lord knows it too. And if I didn't know folks, Mister Jake, I'd stay. I would."

Then she was gone.

It was a little while and then he was quiet. He picked up the napkin again and made a stab at his nose. Then he went to bed. Then he got up and came back into the room and blew out the candle. Then he went back to bed again, stumbling in the dark.

In the morning there was bread and butter and milk again. He ate it. Afterward, he put the dishes into the bucket of water, pulled them out again, and put them onto the drainboard. In a little while he went out across the yard to the privy, and on his way back to the house, he fed the chickens. He was standing in the bedroom, looking down at the dirt covering his pants, when someone came into the room behind him. When he turned around, the man said, "How do, Jake. Earl Metcalf. We uptown decided the thing to do was me to take that cow over to my barn and bring you milk every evenin'. You just ain't going to be able to take care of no cow." Then he saw the man go out to the barn and presently walk away, waving the cow before him.

It was when he had gotten hungry again and eaten all the jelly and crackers that he noticed the dirt again. After a bit, he suddenly sat down and got all his clothes off. Two buttons fell off his shirt onto the floor. He got down on his knees and put his finger on one button and pushed it around awhile; then he was finally able to curl it up under his fingertip and slip it into the palm of his hand. He did that with the other button and wadded up his shirt with the buttons inside it. He found clothes like those he had taken off and he got them on, except for his shirttail, which trailed out. Then he started uptown, the wadded-up shirt carefully beneath his arm. He walked slowly at first, but by the time he entered town he had again hit his high, loping stride. When someone spoke to him, he made some sort of sound in return, opened his mouth wide and grinned.

When he entered the store, the woman said: "We were talking 'bout you just now, Jake. Come on in." Someone near the Coke case handed him a cold bottle. "I got a boy that's going to bring you down some groceries every week for fifteen cents," Miss Loma said. "Then I'll send a little bill up to the bank in Senatobia every week, and they'll pay me out of the little money your momma left."

"He don't understand all that talk," said a man sucking on a toothpick.

"I know it," the woman said. "But I feel like I ought to speak it out in public in case there's ever any question about the money. You know how the government is."

"That's right," said another lady. She handed Jake a package of Nabs. "And somebody will be taking him a little cooked something now and then. I declare, look at him. He's got on clean clothes and looks almost decent as she kept him."

"What's that — a shirt? What's he want?" said the man, wiggling his toothpick to the other side.

He offered the shirt again; this time the woman noticed it. "You reckon he wants it washed?" Miss Loma said. She took the shirt and opened it, and the buttons fell onto the floor. He began to nod his head. "Look, you reckons it's the buttons?" she said. She picked them up and said, "You want the buttons back on, Jake?" She looked at the others. "Yes, I believe that's what he wants. I'll do 'em and wash it," she said. "You come back for it in a few days."

"Now, can you beat that?" the other lady said. "Jake, you got any more sewing, you bring it in. We in the Baptist Thursday Club can all take turns doing it."

One by one those who came to the store left again. He sat for a long time on a nail keg near the door. He ate what was given to him and grinned at those who spoke to him. Occasionally someone would say, "You ain't crazy, are you, Jake? But you ain't far from it!" and then they would slap him on the back, and he would grin very wide at them. They would say then, "You're all right, boy!"

Miss Loma said, "Closing time, Jake. Early on Wednesdays." He went out the screen door when she held it open. There was hardly anyone in town when he walked through, but those who were there all spoke to him. The filling station was still open, but the last car drove away as he passed by, and the owner disappeared into his house next door. A chicken ran ahead of him in the middle of the road, and he *whoosed* at it; from out of sight someone called, "You git him, Jake."

Then he was turning off the main road and going down the road that led past all houses and on into the silence of the countryside and finally to his own gate. He came up to it and looked ahead at the quiet house. When he entered it, no one was there. No one came all afternoon. When the chickens began to make a racket in the yard, he went out and fed them and then he came in and ate on the baloney and the bread Miss Loma had given him. He found a little pail of milk on the table, and he drank that.

It was not long before he noticed the day had lessened; the sun had spread out into long, runny streaks of red and gold, and the persimmon trees began to darken against the horizon. He took his chair out onto the lean-to porch and propped in it against the house, his feet hooked between the rungs. He waited for dark, the candle already in his hand, the match laid carefully by. He knew how to give it one good strike and afterward stick the head into the bucket of water. It was almost time to light the candle when he saw the birds again, hovering over the line of trees before they settled into them out of sight. In the garden the weeds had grown, and dark came early in the tall grass. Once he thought he saw movement there, and he leaned forward quietly looking — he thought what moved might be a dog — but he saw nothing but darkness again, and settled back in his same position.

When full dark came, he lit the candle and went indoors. He took off his clothes tonight and lay flat with a sheet up over him when the candle was out.

Usually he went to sleep quickly. Tonight he lay awake. He looked at his clothes lying in a heap on the floor in the moonlight, and in the quiet and dark gradually understood, as much as he could, that no one was going to stay here again. He was completely alone.

He lay awake as the night and its silence deepened. He had always known silence, but suddenly he was afraid of it. He sat up, startled, and with one terrified but reassuring cry called out at the top of his lungs, telling them all, telling everybody, the one thing in the world he did know fully: that as deep as his own silence was, it was nowhere near so deep as hers.

No Love for the Lonely

*Y*ou sure that clock isn't slow?" Cotter said, laying down his cards.

"I am," his sister said. "It's twenty after seven all over town. You just got to wait to hear your precious Ranch Boys."

It was after supper, and they were playing honeymoon bridge. Cotter sighed and picked up his hand again. "I bid two clubs."

"Clubs?" she said. "I don't see how you're bidding clubs."

Looking down, he saw he had meant to say spades; he was too busy thinking about the program. "You bid your hand, I'll bid mine," he said.

"How can I," she said, "when you're taking my bid?"

"I'm going to turn on the radio," he said.

"Well, turn it low," she said. "I can't listen to the radio and play cards too."

He got up and went over and began fiddling with the dials. Just then she said, "Well, I never."

Something about the way she said it made him turn around. She was sitting straight up, foaming at the mouth a little. "Ruth Edna?" he said, and at that moment saw life so obviously leave her it was like something he could touch. "Ruth Edna," he said again, all he could think of to say.

In the silence following, he heard his own difficult breathing. He sank onto the bed beside her chair and took her hand, wondering if she did not feel cheated too; he had always been the sick one. Her hand lying in his was large, rough, agespotted; if he could have cried over anything, it would have been over the defenseless way the hand lay in his. He patted it reassuringly, knowing if he had only done that in life sometime, things might have been different between him and Ruth Edna. With her not yapping at him and so helpless-looking, her mouth hanging open that way, he felt the hard knot of dislike he had held so long begin to unloosen.

He got up and crossed to the window. Maybe everything hadn't been her fault; maybe he'd been some to blame, he thought, and rubbed the pane clear of his breath to look out. Daylight was taking its time to die, had burned the sky brilliantly red and yellow, all the various shades of roses. At the window an oak bent and scratched the pane, freed itself of two leaves, and they skidded off into the early October evening. He'd need a sweater to go for help; the house had no phone.

Turning to the room, he avoided the chair where she sat and caught sight of the radio, warmed up but soundless. He was sorry to do it but crossed over and turned up the sound. He had waited eight weeks for the Ranch Boys to play his request, to read his name out over the air.

His winter clothes were still packed away. He went about the house searching for his old green cardigan, in the tops of closets, in the drawers of rickety chiffoniers, staying always within range of the Boys' nasal voices and the relentless twang of their guitars. He was on tiptoe, his fingertips walking a box off a high shelf, when the announcer said at last, " 'Hand Me Down My Walking Cane,' for Cotter May!" In a frenzy the Boys tore into their music.

[64]

The box dropped onto his head, spilling clothes and moth-balls in a circle about him. Pride soared like a balloon, and he ran toward the front room, about to call, having forgotten until he saw her. Then he sank into the nearest chair, his arms hanging like weights over the sides, his knuckles as white as marrow on his clenched hands. Looking at her once, he wished for the first time in his life that she would say something.

In the silence he heard all there was left him to hear, a clock ticking and some fool blabbing on the radio. To have his name read out without even Ruth Edna to hear was noth-ing. To hear sound at all was nothing compared to the pro-found silence opposite. He had to leave, found his sweater, and was all the way to the road before he got it on.

An odor of mothballs lessened the smell of evening. Sorrow rose as he thought of the spring afternoon when Ruth Edna had laid the sweater away. He had come into the room as she was stooping, flush-faced, over a box of old clothes he thought were for throwing away — turned out they were the ones she was keeping. Taking a startled look at himself in the mirror, he had seen that that was the way he looked, worn out. No doubt about it. He had tried to pull in his stomach but found it past help. He had studied only his near-baldness without surprise. He had been studying that a good many years, day and night, brushing and arranging the hair that was left. Each night Ruth Edna had raved on about its being the silliest thing she ever heard, any man fixing his hair before going to bed. He'd always meant to ask what difference it made to her. He had been surprised that night to find himself so splay-footed and dumpy, had taken his hands from his pockets, given himself a final going-over, and at that moment abandoned himself to old age. From then on he had seemed always in his own way; he shuffled, and his feet stumbled into each other. No matter how carefully he dressed, his clothes disarranged themselves. He took on, to himself at least, a certain smell — not of uncleanliness or anything like that; musty-smelling, he described it.

Turning from the mirror, he had seen Ruth Edna take his sweater and throw it into the box. "There's that old thing," she had said, madder than usual for no reason he could see. "Oh, I wish I could buy a whole new suitcase full of pretty clothes and go off on a wonderful trip. Go off on one of those great big boats across the ocean."

"Whew, you'd be scared to cross all that water," he had said, and she half screamed, "I would not! I'd go anywhere to get away from here and you."

"Why don't you throw some of those old clothes away?" he had said. It didn't look as though he'd get another year's wear out of much but the sweater anyway.

"Oh," she had said. "Get out!" And when he did, she had followed him all the way down the breezeway to call, "Baggy pants!"

He had looked over his shoulder into a mirror in his own room and had seen he had lost so much weight from the sickness in his chest, his pants did bag.

Tonight, stopping in the near-dark, he gazed beyond an outline of giant trees up to a little house set way off the road; Hattie McGaha's. She and Ruth Edna were all the friends each one had; he knew he ought to go tell her Ruth Edna was gone. But Hattie would weep and wail, and at the moment he felt he couldn't take it. She would recount how Ruth Edna's whole life had been so sad, and he felt danged if he hadn't heard that recently enough from the horse's mouth. He went on, but near the end of the walk stopped to look back at the shack, as he called it. One weak light burned at the rear, like a hermit's place. With a knot in his stomach, he realized he was alone now too.

He was on his way to Wilroy's, his closest friend's, and it seemed suddenly a long way. He left the unsteady wooden walk and made his way in the road; he kept his mind on the sounds of his feet on the gravel and on the wind through the shedding trees. As he approached the house, the lights went off, except for one in Wilroy and Mary Margaret's bedroom. He stood where the light spilled out the window and lay like a yellow blanket across the dark ground. Mary Margaret passed by the window, turning down the bed for the night. He shut his eyes, lulled by the thought of sleep on sheets that were clean and white. When he opened them, it was to the thought of Ruth Edna's frequent and ungentle reminder: "Mary Margaret don't want you dropping in on them unexpectedly all the time; married folks got their own things to themselves." He felt, even with his important news, that he oughtn't to knock now that Mary Margaret had on her nightgown. Even though he had known them all their lives, had been there when they married and when their boy was born, he felt himself a stranger, always looking on.

He moved from the light and toward the house, the night huge around him. The smell of the countryside where he had lived all his life seemed different, the trees near him so gigantic as to be frightening; the dark roads beyond had all been trod by him before, but now they went places he had no need to go, and the yellowed windows of the town's houses framed scenes in which he had no part. If he had had the courage of his desire, he would have run home through the dark, flung his arms about Ruth Edna, and asked forgiveness for all their life together. Surely she was not dead. Not gone! The only thing in the world he had to love. He crouched against the dark, afraid of an insect calling near him, the sorrow so heavy in his chest there was no way he could present it to them.

At his knock Wilroy opened the door, hurrying his striped pajama top into the bottoms. "What're you doing here this time of evening?" he said, and when he heard, he shouted. "Woman! Get in here."

Running through the door full-breasted in her white flannel nightgown, Mary Margaret was like a huge white hen. When she heard, she took Cotter to her and released him only when Wilroy said, "Get the man a drink of whiskey."

Cotter sat in the hall, the whiskey burning away the lining of his stomach, and told how it happened. But all the time he spoke, he wanted to interrupt himself to ask, "Who did that? Who died?" because never in his wildest thoughts had he considered outliving Ruth Edna. When he finished, they sat back, silenced by the enormity of what could happen in only a minute. He thought of the way she had looked foaming at the mouth and said, "Whatever else you want to say about it, there isn't any dignity in death."

Shock deepened in Mary Margaret's face, and he thought, *she's gone fifty-five years thinking life is pretty.* He now paid his first respects to his dead sister, who had known it was not. Looking at Mary Margaret, he was surprised to see she was no longer the young girl he had seen married; she was a middle-aged woman. It didn't seem fair for Ruth Edna to be dead, knowing what she did, and for this woman to be alive, thinking life was a way it was not. He thought of telling how selfish a man could be, of how he had turned up the radio. He would have told if she had not looked across at him with pity just then; he was afraid of losing that.

He allowed Wilroy to pour him another drink he shouldn't take, suddenly envying Ruth Edna's not having to decide things anymore: what she wanted or did not want, what was right or wrong. He fought the whiskey into a stomach that did not want it, knowing how wrong it had been for him to turn up the program. He put away in his mind the fact that he had, hoping he would forget it.

Wilroy telephoned the doctor in Whitehill. "Well, sir," he said after he hung up, "everything's taken care of," and he slapped Cotter on the shoulder.

Mary Margaret said, "You got to spend the night here now, you hear?" and he was lulled again by the thought of the clean sheets. He could see their bed, with an impression where someone had sat. He seemed to have gazed at the bed in some other life, misted over by darkness. He squinted against the hall light, elbows on his thighs, his hands hanging between them, a drink clutched in one. He looked at the buxom woman standing over him, and raising his glass, said, "Won't you join us, Miss Ma' Margaret?"

"Why, Cotter May!" she said, not knowing whether to laugh or not.

Wilroy did laugh. "Get the man another drink of whiskey, woman. What's the matter with you?"

"She want us to die of thirst?" Cotter said, drinking elaborately and laughing with Wilroy. He saw in Wilroy's eyes a message that he had seen there before; because of a certain dizziness, he could not remember where and surprised himself by saying, "That was a long time ago."

"It's been a long time," Wilroy said. And then Cotter left him, was taken away on the most wonderful waves of sleep he had known since he was a boy. In sleep he remembered that the umbrella he had looked for all summer was in Wilroy's hall closet. Ruth Edna appeared, saying, "Where's the umbrella? You lost it! I've never seen anybody like you in my life. You *always* lose umbrellas." And he said, "Hush up, woman." And she did.

The town reacted to Ruth Edna's death much as he had expected: surprised, solicitous. The funeral went off without his doing hardly anything. And everyone came, whether they cared about Ruth Edna or not. When he looked into the casket, he could not get over her appearance; she was real as life. The undertaker had even left the tiny lines of dissatisfaction around her mouth, and he wished those had been taken away — as if, at last, she had found a place she wanted to be.

When everyone had had a look and taken a seat, he stood alone before the casket, shielded from view by the pallbearers. He lifted the netting and gingerly touched Ruth Edna's face, then jumped back, shocked by her coldness — though, of course, he had known she would be cold. He took his seat but did not hear a single word of the whole burial service. All he could think of was the tip of his finger almost burning a hole in his pants with its coldness, as if he had just touched hot ice. His throat burned with the salty taste of withheld tears.

For the rest of his life, at the mention of Ruth Edna's name, his whole being was flooded with this sense of burning and with the overly sweet, sickroom smell of too many day lilies; the ladies of the church had picked their yards clean.

During the first weeks after his bereavement, life was a whirl such as it had never been before. Somebody invited him to supper every night. The preacher had him at noontime, except on Sundays, when Mary Margaret never failed him. Between eating engagements he developed the habit of dropping in to see her and Wilroy. He began to associate the three of them in his mind. When he said "we," he assumed that whoever he was talking to knew whom he meant. He thought of himself as a familiar figure in town passing along the walk between their house and his. It had got so he could stop

Hattie's many invitations by a mere nod of his head toward Wilroy's. She did not even come down to the road anymore, just sat rocking on her porch, watching him pass.

The fifth Sunday after his loss it occurred to him Mary Margaret had not spoken about dinner. Hesitating, he decided the invitation was taken for granted and set off happily through the chilly noon, glad he had on a suit coat over the green cardigan, only briefly embarrassed when church let out as he passed. As long as Brother Patrick had had him to meals, he had attended regularly. Possessed by the devil, he greeted elaborately Miss Maudie Mae Boone, who tottered toward him, Bible tucked under her arm. Coming behind her, Hattie shot her eyebrows up and her hat slid over them. Cotter smiled, passing, thinking the hat must have been one of the things of Ruth Edna's she'd come for, and it was too big.

He approached Wilroy's bursting with greetings; then something cold as death clutched his heart. A Memphis car stood in the drive. Wilroy's boy and his family down for the day! Dodging behind shrubbery, he watched as they rounded a corner of the house and went inside. Over the young mother's shoulder a baby's tiny white face dangled like a broken flower; the lump in Cotter's throat felt as large. He did not know how long he hid there feeling like some dumb animal before he lifted his nose to the smell of chicken frying, imagining he could smell even the biscuits in the oven. He thought of the big old dining room with its centered table in shadows, though the noon sun was at every window. The crystal centerpiece would be full of roses, and the starched white tablecloth would shine at the places where so many elbows had worn it thin. He thought of lemon pie, heavily meringued.

The quiet was broken by a sound like the tinkling of many small bells. Grace having been said, everyone at once stirred sugar into his iced tea. Without having to look, Cotter knew the time was exactly 12:15. He hadn't been asked; all it meant was he wasn't wanted. Something more disturbed him. He walked away, thinking it would come to him.

His nose was tickled by the smell of the tiny rambler roses growing over Hattie's fence. He broke off a branch and went up to her porch. She was not in sight, and he sat down, hoping she had not eaten yet. Presently she appeared, puffing up the hill from the privy. When he presented the flowers, she said, "Looks like the late-blooming rambler down by my gate, don't it?" and tucked the branch into a milk bottle already full of them.

"Well, Hattie," he said, rocking back reflectively, noting when she sat down that her little black-clad feet barely reached the floor. "How're you?"

She scootched, one hip after the other, to the back of her chair; then her feet hung without touching anything, toes down. "I'm doing all right, Cotter," she said, watching her hands press out the lap of her dress.

"Well," he said. He rocked, sucking at an empty space between his teeth.

They watched cars pass in the road. Clouds were forming just beyond the heavy pink arch of roses; there was a sound in the sky, the first hint of thunder. "Looks like rain," Hattie said.

"Looks like it," Cotter said.

"Cotton got burned all summer," she said. "Farmers sure need it."

"Sure do." He rocked on silently until his stomach conveniently rumbled.

"You eat?" she said.

"As a matter of fact, I ain't," he said. "You?"

"Law, I hardly fix meals anymore," she said. "Eatin' by

myself all the time. I just pick here and there. Had me a cup
of tea a little while ago." She slid from the chair and went
off to the kitchen. He rocked on, watching the Sunday-
afternoon riders pass on the road. Soon he began to feel sort
of comfortable and at home smelling dinner in the kitchen;
his hurt from Wilroy had eased, and he tried to look at the
matter straight. What had really bothered him was their not
even thinking of him, just going ahead with their own plans.
When Hattie called him to the table and they sat down, she
said, "This always happens, Cotter."

"What's that?" he said.

She said, "Folks crowd around after trouble when you don't
know your head from your hind end. Then about the time
you get yourself straightened out and ready to see them,
they're off busy with their own selves again."

It was on his tongue to say he wasn't finding that so at all,
that he was as busy as could be. But suddenly he saw the
two of them sitting there in that falling-down kitchen with
their poor worn-out bodies in poor worn-out clothes and their
old eyes watering and squinting at each other across their
plates of canned meat, and he knew the moment called for
truth. He acknowledged it by remaining silent.

They digested the rest of the afternoon, rocking. By evening
he felt regretful about having to go. He walked slowly, dread-
ing the empty house and the rooms almost as Ruth Edna had
left them. Dust blew across the floor when he opened the
front door. He tried to hear in the silence that welcomed him
an echo, a voice from the past, tried to make his memories
bring the house alive, but he could not. He came farther into
the room, as cluttered and filthy as the kinds of places police
found strange old people dead in, with fortunes hidden in
stacks of newspapers. Only they weren't going to find one
in this mess, he thought, kicking aside yesterday's clothes.

And that was the whole point. They weren't going to find anything interesting at all.

He passed the hours in his room, rocking, the wick of the lamp turned sky-high, the house about him dark and silent, with Ruth Edna's idle things and her smell still about it. He was remorseful, wishing he had asked once in her life what now seemed so easy: "What'n the world you want, Ruth Edna? To get married?"

He was sitting too close to the high lamplight. His forehead and the sparse gray hairs of his chest were beaded with sweat. He pressed his hand against the hollow that was his chest, able to feel his lungs searching for air. His body had long ago sagged with the hopelessness of recovering its lost strength, but now a latent manly thought stirred him: He had missed the best of life.

Deep in the night he woke to hear a rising wind heavy in the branches of the oak, to smell dust blowing in from the road. As a child, at the heralding of rain, he would kneel in the road excitedly, awaiting the first pockings in the soft yellow dust. He was fond of storm smell and could bring it to mind anytime he wanted, the way he could the undone things of his past. Excitement swelled in him, and he lay, gripped by a desire to taste, before it was altogether too late, what life was all about.

He remembered Wilroy asking him once if he was ever going to marry. They had been in a bottom, cutting wood. He had looked around at the lush greenness, terrified at the thought, and passed the remark off lightly. "Who'd have a old bachelor like me?" he had said.

"Hattie would," Wilroy had said. "With pleasure."

"Hattie?" he had said, surprised.

"Are you blind as well as dumb, boy?" Wilroy had said,

and that had been the end of it till now, twenty years later when, waking in the night, he wondered if she still would.

Wilroy had said, "You ought to marry and get free."

"Free?" he had said. "Married *and* free?"

"Yes," Wilroy had said. "Free."

Cotter had turned away then, suddenly loyal to Ruth Edna. Despite their friendship, his silence had remained between him and Wilroy all these years, and now he sat up, knowing that the message in Wilroy's eyes the night Ruth Edna died had been "Free at last."

Early in the morning he got out the old lawn mower. He was already cutting the grass when Wilroy came by on his way to town for the mail. "What'n the name of Holy are you doing, Cotter?" he said, leaning against the fence.

"Trying to get this place in some kind of shape," Cotter said, and Wilroy had to catch him and half carry him up to the porch. He pushed him into a chair.

"Cotter May, you take the cake," he said. "I never seen you cut grass before."

"Before I got on my deathbed," Cotter said, and had to draw in deeply to find the breath to say it.

"Naw, boy," Wilroy said.

"This cough is a booger, Wilroy." He tried to sit so that he could breathe easier. "I believe it's trying to kill me. I sure do."

"Pshaw, young man like you?" Wilroy said. "I wish I was five years younger like you." He winked toward several young girls passing by in short socks and even shorter skirts, heading uptown.

Embarrassed, Cotter could not look after their slim waists and little round behinds. He thought of Hattie, raillike, safe in her long black skirt. He tried to take Wilroy's mind back to that day in the bottom and was surprised Wilroy did not remember it. He had to plunge ahead then, tomato-red, and explain his new philosophy. He ended by saying, "You reckon Hattie would still have me?"

Wilroy looked as if Cotter had suddenly punched him in the stomach. Openmouthed, he said, "Why, boy, we'll sure get Miss Mary Margaret to find out." He said good-bye, and he'd be seeing him, and it sure wasn't true you couldn't teach an old dog new tricks; and they laughed and shook hands. Cotter felt Wilroy had a new respect for him, that a warmness flowed between them that never had been there before. He went to bed with qualms that Hattie would not have him. The thought gave him the same feeling of excited anticipation that waiting for his name on the radio had.

But before he had had his coffee next morning, Hattie was there with her answer. "Oh, Cotter," she said, hands trembling toward her hair. "Who'd have thought about us getting together after all these years?" Her withered cheeks bloomed like fall apples. Unmoved, Cotter looked at her, thinking it was too bad he had cheated her of love when she was young. She looked silly, and as he sipped the coffee she had made too strong, he thought maybe now was too late after all.

Mary Margaret came, crying happily, "Cotter May, I declare to my soul!" before she and Hattie tore into Ruth Edna's house, glad to have their hands on it at last.

Cotter got a pain in his chest and retired to the shadows of his room. Over his rocker's squeakings he could hear them thumping and bumping and twittering all over the house. He wished they would go home. And the terrible thought occurred that if he married Hattie, this was home; she would never leave.

At noon Hattie brought him food on a tray and stood timidly, then fled at the thunderous look on his face. He pushed away the one thin sandwich on the tray, deciding to sulk, and stared at himself in a gold-framed photograph on the dresser; he was young, broad-shouldered, and was kneeling with his arms around the necks of Old Dan and Pat, his hounds. For a week he had cried secretly, completely broken, after each of their deaths. If he were still that man, he thought, with a brief hand wave toward the picture, they wouldn't dare bring him a dinner looking like a ladies' tea party. His spirit rose, walked through the house and told them, *I want something hot! Meat and potatoes and gravy. What's the matter with you?* but his body had no intention of moving out of the impression it had worn into the old down pillow on the rocker.

Later Mary Margaret appeared in the doorway, dusting herself off, and said, "Cotter, you're not going to even recognize this place. I got to go get Wilroy's supper now, but I'll see you tomorrow."

He had smelled cabbage cooking for some time; now he smelled chops frying, and presently Hattie called him. He followed the smells resentfully, carrying the empty tray, resenting that too; he had got so hungry in the afternoon that he had eaten the sandwich.

Sooty and frail, Hattie set a plate before him and tried to smile. Somehow she could not seem to manage to get everything onto the table, and he had almost finished eating before she sat down. But her sitting there gave him a chance to look closely at the house he was not going to recognize. And he didn't. His own house. Everything was changed. The hearth he thought was black had been scrubbed until it was, surprisingly, an old red brick. On the mantel were no longer arranged the few souvenirs of life Ruth Edna had cared about: a toy elephant with a trunk long enough to say GREETINGS FROM GREAT SMOKY MTS. NAT'L PARK, a celluloid doll with hair of silver sprinkles and a skirt of green feathers, and artificial flowers — so real you couldn't tell the difference — bought in Rock City, near Chattanooga. In their place was his collection of African violets in white pots he had particularly wanted ranged along the floor in the front room to catch the morning sun. The late-afternoon light was different in the kitchen, too; he had to squint to look around. The dark green shades he and Ruth Edna had favored were gone. Everything of hers was gone, and he thought it must all be packed in the boxes lined along the breezeway.

The night was pitch-dark before Hattie finished washing dishes and joined him in the front room. He had a little fire going and was sitting in a rocker brought up before it. She almost sat in the other one, Ruth Edna's, and they both started. She drew it aside and brought up a small cane chair from against the wall.

Cotter was disappointed in himself for not saying what he knew she expected. He had not even answered when she said, "Wilroy told me what you told him to say about you trying to fix up the yard. I declare, Cotter, it was mighty sweet."

He watched out of the corner of his eye as she stretched her worn shoes toward the fire. And he knew it was never going to work. He didn't have enough time left to have his violets and his whole life rearranged. He was old, and he was cold, and he wanted a comforter across his knees without having to tell anybody. Hattie, he saw, had let the fire go out. In short, he wanted Ruth Edna back after spending almost his whole life wanting her gone. None of this would have happened if Wilroy hadn't badgered him that time, in the bottom, about getting married.

He was startled, waking, to find that he had slept. Hattie stood before him, feeling for her flashlight in the embroidered knitting bag she always carried. He saw by her face that she understood life was withholding this last promise, as it had withheld so many others: that it had all been too good to be true.

When she had gone, he thought of her bent figure walking through the night, alone from now on with nothing to look forward to, in that shack every night eating cold supper, saving kerosene by using one lamp; him, the same. It was too bad they would have to sit half a mile apart, suffering their loneliness, but he could not come out of himself after all these years. He huddled into himself even more after almost emerging, regretting it had been for one day only that he had almost been a man.

Looking around the shadowed room, his eyes came to the radio. He went over and turned it on. Then he sat down again and pulled the other rocker to him. When it was in place, he turned to it and said, "You know what I think I'm going to do, Ruth Edna? I'm going to write the Ranch Boys again."

Going Ahead

*I*N the middle of the city was a park, on Main Street, a square; there, inside a hut, Santa Claus sat, with a heater to warm him. Tad stood in line with the other children thinking what he would do; go in one door, speak to Santa, receive candy, come out on the side where the grown-ups waited. He could tell his grandfather was cold waiting, and he was cold too. Children around him wore rubber boots, though it was not raining; his grandfather said later it was because of the cold and the frost slowly melting, leaving the grass wet. He had on the everyday, heavy work boots he wore even to the barn. Usually, to Delton, he wore Sunday-school shoes, but his mother had said she did not care if they called him "country," if he looked country; he had to be warm. He had not admitted that his shoes made no difference; he always felt country arriving, bouncing along in the cab of the dusty or muddy pickup, looking down on everyone. City people in ordinary cars sped by below or, worse, crawled impatiently behind, waiting to pass. Once he had asked his grandfather, "Can we ever get a car?"

And Grandpa had said, "A pickup's always served us. Why change?"

Another time Grandpa had said, "Boy, damn if you ain't

got big enough for me to carry to Delton by yourself. I been waiting a long time. In the springtime, we'll go up yonder to a ball game and the zoo. Now, I reckon I'll have to carry you to see Santa."

He had planned the trip with Grandpa ever since he could remember, but his father had said, "Poppa, you and the boy don't have any business going up there to Delton. There's too many things happening on the highway with the Negroes bothering folks in Mississippi cars."

His grandfather had said, "I'm not going to bother none of them, why are they going to bother me?"

"Because you're white," his mother had said, turning from the stove; then his father had said, "That's exactly right." But Tad had said nothing.

He had watched his father and Grandpa get ready to go to the barn to milk. His father had stomped into a boot and said, "I don't know what you want to go for anyway. I hear the Negroes have taken over downtown Delton. Everything's integrated. Things have changed, Poppa. You're going to have to realize it."

Grandpa had said, "I've never had any trouble with Negroes. I don't expect to start now. Ain't any of them going to bother an old man and a little boy on the highway."

He had known his mother would tell the story again. She had said, "Ellie Watkins was driving back and saw a pickup on her tail. She slowed to let it pass, but it wouldn't. So, she went faster, but it did. Went on down the highway that way, until finally it did go by, flying. She wanted to get home then and went faster too. Suddenly the truck came almost to a stop, in the middle of the road. No reason in the world, except to make her bump it. She skidded so, she said sparks came out of her tires. As soon as she got stopped, the truck went

[84]

on. It turned off onto a side road and when she passed, she saw three Negro boys looking back at her, dying laughing."

"If you're bound and determined, Poppa, you, number one, put that pistol in the glove compartment and, two, be back here before dark, and I mean plumb before," his father had said before going out with Grandpa. He had thought they looked like giants the way they were huddled into their outdoor clothes. They had opened the door, and cold had come in and traveled the room like a whisper before the fire warmed it again after they went out. He had hugged his knees. "Mother," he had said, "can I tell Grandpa I don't believe in Santa Claus anymore?"

"Goodness, no," she had said. "You'll spoil his fun. You can pretend, can't you?"

"Sure," he had said.

This morning he had had no chores. He and Grandpa ate leftover corn bread with sorghum, and then they started. His wool gloves were worn at the ends, and his fingers had felt frozen when he came into the morning. It was twenty miles over a winding gravel road to the main highway, then fifty more over blacktop to Delton, into Tennessee. He and Grandpa had lost time looking for the pistol; then his mother had remembered it was already in the truck. She went nowhere without it, though in north Mississippi there had been no serious trouble since things had been settled at the university. But his mother had said there was a differentness: beneath their ordinary lives there was a feeling of waiting, of always wondering if something would happen.

For the first time in his life — Grandpa said for the first time in *his* — people locked their doors. If his mother went for a loaf of bread, she shut up the house. His grandfather said folks had went crazy; they ought to remember what FDR had said about being afraid. His mother had said locking doors made strangers; it was as if they all hid something from each other; she was afraid to express her views anymore; you didn't know how the other fellow would react to what you thought. He thought that all grown-ups thought about was change. His father had said they had to go along with it, the best they could.

This morning nothing had happened on the highway. Cars with Negroes had passed, and no one paid any attention to him and Grandpa. Once, a car ahead of them had slowed and a farmer turned into a field, a Negro helper sitting beside him. "You see any trouble there?" Grandpa had said.

"No," he had said, and looking into Grandpa's eyes had been like looking into the cistern: he had seen himself reflected. His grandfather's eyes, his hair, his mustache were all the same silver-gray color as the flat, still water. They had gone on, looking at a sun so pale it was hardly distinguishable from the white winter sky.

Now, waiting to see Santa Claus, he stood warming his hands, squeezing them and pulling the ends of his gloves longer, the way Grandpa had taught him. Behind him a girl spoke, her breath jumping in spurts like steam, telling another child the lake at the zoo was expected to freeze; people could skate there. He tried to imagine ice-skating, wondering if the pond behind his house would freeze; he had no skates if it did. Long ago winters in Mississippi had been very cold. Grandpa had skated every year on the pond behind the house, and Tad tried now to imagine him as a little boy.

Santa Claus called him, and he stepped over the doorsill into the hut. Immediately, warming, his fingers were full of pain. He wondered how the man stood it so hot with all that stuff on his face, and why he painted his nose red. Was that what little children expected? If he had to pretend for Grandpa's sake, he would have to pretend for the man's too, he had decided. He shook hands, looking the man in the eye, as Grandpa always said to, and said, "How do, Santa Claus."

"Have you been a good boy this year?" the man said.

"Yes, sir. I guess so," he said.

"What can I bring you?"

"A twenty-two," he said. "Single-shot."

"I'll have to ask your mother and daddy about that, son. Maybe when you're older."

"I've used my dad's a year," he said. "I killed a moccasin on the back steps, and there's always something after the chickens."

"Keep on being a good boy then," the man said. "Here's a little gift. Come in, little girl. Come and see old Santa." Tad turned toward the exit and stepped out, holding the candy cane, glad he was small for his age, and hoping no one else would know he was nine.

As soon as he was out, Grandpa said, "How was old Santa?" He said, "Fine."

"He don't keep you in there long," Grandpa said.

"I reckon he's trying to hurry folks out of the cold," he said.

"I reckon so," Grandpa said, feeling better. "What'd you want?"

He said, "A twenty-two," and knew he was getting the gun from the way Grandpa gave a little bounce. "Uh-huh," Grandpa said. "What else?"

"Shells," he said.

"For shore. You need a gun, you need some shells," Grandpa said. "You asking for anything else?" Tad knew the shells were bought too. He had nothing else in mind, but suddenly he said, "Grandpa, if the pond freezes over, can I get ice skates?"

[87]

They walked on, Grandpa pulling his scarf tighter. "Well," Grandpa said. "We'll have to see."

He knew there would be nothing to see. His father would say: "Son, if we had the money, just to throw away, I'd get you the skates in a minute. But that pond might stay frozen one, two, at the most three days and never freeze again." He knew that made sense, but anything he mentioned, Grandpa would bear in mind. Once he had overheard his grandfather say, "The closest I'll ever come to heaven is watching that boy grow up." Tad had felt a sudden huge swelling in his chest. He had that feeling now, walking beside Grandpa, knowing he was worrying over how to get him something. "Grandpa," he said, "we better forget about the skates. That pond might stay froze a day or two and never freeze again."

"That's so," Grandpa said. But a tag end of thought seemed, still, to remain in his mind.

They chose first to pass the peanut man who stood outside the Planters shop wearing a plastic peanut head, carrying a cane, and passing out a spoonful of nuts to anyone who held out a hand. He and Grandpa could not understand those who did not. "Nothing like goobers," Grandpa said, tossing peanuts into his mouth.

"Nothing like goobers," he said, tasting fuzz from his wool glove with them.

Grandpa could not understand parking meters but would not spend money on a lot. Now, as they were passing their truck, Grandpa gave him the dimes and he punched in two for two hours and tried to explain. Still Grandpa said he could not understand those machines and walked away shaking his head and said, "We got to get your momma's and daddy's presents. Eat some dinner, look at toys, then get on home early like we promised. What you got in mind for your daddy?"

"I don't know," he said. "What does he need?"

Grandpa said, as always, "He could use something to hep him if he gets snake-bit."

Every year they bought his father a bottle of rye together. His father opened the present as if in surprise and said how glad he was to have his supply of snake-bite medicine replenished. Then Grandpa would say he had thought he was about to run out; even if they didn't use whiskey much, when you needed a drink, you needed it. Last Christmas, Grandpa had said, "You never know. This boy's liable to be coming in here any day now telling us he's got married. We'd have to drink to that."

"Shoot!" Tad had said, "I'm never going to get married."

"Why, what about the little redheaded girl I saw you walking along the road with?" Grandpa had said.

"Her!" he had said, and this past year had gotten off the school bus early never to have to get off with the little redheaded girl again.

Where he lived, whiskey was sold only by bootleggers — Baptists had voted the county dry — and he followed Grandpa into the liquor store with a sense of guilt. But Grandpa stepped straight up to the counter and said, "We'd like to take us a fifth of Four Roses, please, sir."

On the counter Tad put a dollar of the two he had in change. The storekeeper brought the bottle and swiftly, with one finger, separated the coins spread on the counter and counted them again. "Dollar even, son," he said. "Thank you." Grandpa gave the rest of the money, and the man said, "Merry Christmas."

Grandpa stepped back, onto the foot of a Negro customer, and turning said quickly, "I'm sorry."

"That's all right," the Negro man said. "I wasn't watching myself."

"Merry Christmas," Grandpa said.

"Merry Christmas," the Negro said.

"Merry Christmas, son," the storekeeper said.

He said, "Merry Christmas," and opened the door, and bells jingled.

When they were on the street, Grandpa said, "Well, we got that over with," as if he had not known what to buy.

Tad said, "Now we have to get Mother's presents; that's harder," and he followed Grandpa into another store. They went up and down aisles looking at things they knew ladies liked, and Tad spent his dollar on a small straw basket with a bottle of perfume inside.

Grandpa said, "I think you know more about ladies than I do. You hep me decide." Though the present was not for Tad, his heart beat faster at the idea of spending five dollars. His grandfather always said the money had to be spent on foolishness, meaning something his mother would not buy for herself. He and Grandpa finally decided on pearls that could be worn many ways; the saleslady showed them, hung them in one long strand down her neck, wound them once, then twice around it. "Now that's sho nuff some foolishness," Grandpa said, handing over the money. "We ready to eat dinner now?"

"Can't we see the toys first?" he said.

"Can't you wait?" Grandpa said.

"No," he said; then, in the elevator, Grandpa said, "Boy, I bet your stomach's going to be waiting when you get there."

His mother had said to remember his grandfather was an old man. "You want to rest?" he said, but Grandpa said he could go on a while longer. He led Grandpa to the counter where there were toys having to do with space and science. One by one, he picked up models of the latest planes and explained them to Grandpa, who could hardly believe how fast the real ones flew. In one corner of the store was a toy

[90]

spaceship large enough to walk inside. He and Grandpa went in, and he picked up the helmet of a space suit and put it on. "Just think, Grandpa," he said, "when I'm grown, I'll probably be flying to the moon."

"Well, when you learn how to fly this thing, son, take me to the moon with you," Grandpa said.

"Grandpa, you wouldn't go," he said. "You've always said you never wanted your feet that high off the ground."

"I'd take them off for you," Grandpa said. Then he put a helmet on Grandpa's head, and they laughed at each other a long time through the transparent flaps. They decided on the dime store for lunch. It was past the usual eating time when they arrived, and no one else was there. Only one counter was open. Grandpa, sitting down, said he guessed he would have to have some fried clams. His mother had said Grandpa was not supposed to eat fried food. "But if I'm not there, he does," she had said. "I'll bet he comes home sick."

Now Tad said, "You're not supposed to eat fried things," and Grandpa said, "That's just some foolish notion on the doctor's part. What are you going to have?"

"I think I'll have the foot-long hot dog," he said.

When they were eating, Grandpa said the clams were good, even if they had come out of a box, frozen. Tad said the hot dog was good too, but when he bit into one end, mustard squirted out the other. He put his head as far back as possible and licked the bun, hearing other people sit down. When he sat up straight, he saw the other people were Negroes. Grandpa was not eating, and he said, "Are you already sick?"

"No," Grandpa said. "Come on, we've got to go."

"We haven't finished our dinner," he said.

"Come on, we've got to go," Grandpa said and stood up, taking the packages.

He followed Grandpa to the cashier and up the steps and

[91]

out onto the street. Then he said, "Was it the Negroes, Grandpa?" But Grandpa would not say anything; he just kept walking.

In a little while they were in the truck again, moving higher than anyone else, and he said, "You've sat next to Negroes before, Grandpa."

"They've never set to the table with me," Grandpa said.

"They've sat in the truck, close as this," he said.

"They've never set to the table with me," Grandpa said.

"You broke open watermelons and ate them in the field."

Grandpa said in a flat voice, as if something had been taken from him, "They just set right down there, with me."

It was nearly evening when they got back, after driving without speaking between frozen fields over the same road that no longer seemed the same. Lights coming on in houses and barns were like scattered pieces of the fallen pale sun. Doors were shut against the cold; no one was on the road; and it was suppertime. The only store open was where the old men stayed as long as possible to play checkers. Tad looked in, going by, and saw them. Grandpa's friends, he thought. Maybe his father had been right: Grandpa should have stayed at home. When they were at home, Tad told what had happened, and his father said, "We warned you, Poppa."

Grandpa said that he was never going to Delton again; traffic had been so heavy it gave him a nervous stomach; he was going to bed. "Would you bring me some soda?" he asked.

When his grandfather was gone, Tad said, "Grandpa ate fried clams." But when his mother took up the soda she said, "This'll help that old nervous stomach."

"Why does Grandpa eat what he knows will hurt him?" Tad said.

His father said, "He doesn't want to admit he can't do everything he did when he was young."

There were a lot of things Grandpa couldn't admit, Tad thought: what he had eaten, that he was old, that times had changed. And Tad could not tell him he no longer believed in Santa Claus.

His mother said that Tad had had a long day; he had to go to bed.

He went, but he was not sleepy. He lay awake a long time, looking out, studying patterns of the stars against the early night sky, and planning. If Grandpa couldn't change himself enough to go seventy miles to Delton, Tad thought, Grandpa couldn't change himself enough to go to the moon. He would have to go on ahead without him. He guessed he could not tell Grandpa that either.

Pariah

$\mathcal{S}$HE had made a gelatin salad the night before, and this morning, lifting the waxed paper, she shook the mold tentatively. The salad seemed jelled, a success; she had now only to dread the moment of turning the ring onto a platter and prayed it would come out in one piece. With a load of breakfast dishes, the dishwasher seemed to roar, clank, grind more than usual; all together, magnified, its sounds were giving her a headache. She could not think exactly what to do, and if she did not remember and do everything on schedule, she would not be ready for the bridge club. Last-minute flurry would make her go to pieces.

Again she had to open the refrigerator, not remembering whether she had bought cottage cheese to fill the salad's center. In the middle of the dining-room table, which she had set the night before, was a bowl of fruit. Everyone was on a diet, and so dessert was cookies, easy to resist. Overlapping them on a silver tray, she smiled, thinking what Mary Elena would say: "Oh, I wish you hadn't. Don't they look delicious! Let me try just one." And while the others nibbled perhaps one chocolate leaf and dutifully sliced a pear onto their plates or peeled an apple, Mary Elena's fruit would lie untouched, and her hand would go continually — and, she would think,

[97]

surreptitiously — to the cookie tray. When they had eaten and were sitting at the bridge table, Mary Elena would claim innocently that she had been on a diet for months, that she did not understand it, but she could not lose an ounce. If anyone mentioned the cookies, her swollen face would be shocked. "Why, I ate one or two of them, but I didn't have a bite of breakfast."

Placing the last cookie on the tray, Ruth wondered why some people had no willpower and could not see themselves as they were. In the dining room, she set down the tray, proud she did not have any desire for the least chocolate morsel.

Sunlight in the room bounded off snow, making the silverware, the china gleam like foil. She stood still, closing her eyes against a pain that seemed to draw her temples together, as if she had not slept enough; and yet, to terminate an argument with Dean, she had gone to bed earlier than usual. She could no longer remember what the argument had been about or what had started it. Their arguments ran together now into a continuous one, without beginning or end, often leaving her feeling muddled. Dean, she thought, was the argumentative one, and ought not to blame her because the children were being affected.

He came home infrequently now and usually late, but she had been in a good mood when he arrived last night. After dinner with the children, when the dishwasher had been loaded, she had begun to set the table for today; but now, in the bright room, opening heavy eyes, she saw that the knives and forks had been placed wrong and the napkins forgotten. How had she been so confused? Not to be ready made her feel pressured, and she began to tremble, going around the table and straightening the settings. Peter, who was six, had helped her; perhaps he had put everything on wrong. She remembered vaguely that they had spent a long time laughing, though she could not remember now what had been so funny.

As always, Cynthia, who was sixteen, had been in her room with the door closed, supposedly studying. But if she studied as often as the door was closed, she ought to be at the head of her class.

Instead, Ruth had been summoned to school, where Cynthia's adviser said that she seemed in rebellion, had no interest in things, and came to school with her assignments half done or not at all. Ruth, wondering what Cynthia spent her time doing, answered only that she found Cynthia increasingly uncooperative at home too. Perhaps it was being sixteen, she suggested; but the adviser looked doubtful. Could she help Cynthia with her studies? Why, she had barely got through math herself and did not understand this new math at all; she could not even understand Cynthia's English, which had been her own best subject. The adviser agreed that things were taught differently and suggested that if Ruth sat with Cynthia while she studied, showed interest and sympathy, it might help. She could certainly do that, Ruth said, smiling, unable to tell the man that Cynthia would not spend any time with her, not even to shop for clothes. Recently, when they went to a doctor, Cynthia walked ahead down the street, as if she did not want people to know they were together.

The adviser's information disturbed her, and she left him, feeling as nervous as a cat. For the first time in her life, she went into a bar alone, and two martinis gave her confidence. But Cynthia, when she tried to talk to her, gave her a solid, frozen look, as if she hated her.

She bent over to take napkins from a drawer and felt decidedly sick. At forty, she knew too many women having serious operations and would go to a doctor soon. Peter must have been told to put the napkins on and had forgotten. What other explanation could there be for mistakes in the table setting she had gone to bed thinking was perfect? There were no serving spoons and no mayonnaise ladle. Someone, it seemed, had taken things off the table later, to make her feel rattled today.

Then at last, when everything was done, she stood and listened to the house's silence, wondering what she would do next. Outside, in the sun-brightened snow, tiny brown-and-white birds hopped about, and she had the feeling suddenly that, except for Peter, who was young, she was alone. The table's not being right, the house's silence seemed to reproach her, and depression seemed a pendulum hung heavily inside her, ticking away her life. What, she thought, had happened to it? After she played bridge, what would she do until she played bridge again?

Faintly, she recalled that she was singing about loneliness to Peter when Dean arrived last night. Peter was laughing. She was dancing with him about the dining room, holding him at eye level, as if he were her partner, moaning, as a blues singer would, "Who cares for starlit skies — when your lovvv-er has gone," and together they made so much noise that they heard neither Dean's car nor his entrance into the house.

He suddenly stood in the dining room, and she thought he was sick. Pale, with shadows beneath his eyes, he crossed the room in two strides and set Peter down, demanding to know what she was doing with the child up at ten-thirty. Peter, already in pajamas, scuddled away, and she listened to his bedsprings as he jumped into bed. The suddenness of having him snatched away had thrown her against the wall. She remained there, dizzy and panting, but laughing at the fun they had had, at the scare Dean had given her. He had no sense of humor, she said, laughing so hard, still, that she staggered against the dining-room table.

"Go to bed instantly," Dean said.

"Why should I go to bed?" she said proudly and went from the room, upstairs. "Just because you're a square," she said, and, suddenly feeling like yelling, shouted. "A *square* having one drink before dinner doesn't mean other people can't have two. If that's what you're insinuating. I had two tiny martinis, that's all."

Staring up from the bottom of the stairs, he looked old, and she wondered, frightened, if she looked that old. "Go to bed," he repeated, and she went.

She heard Dean come upstairs and go into Cynthia's room, and she waited to hear what they would say. More eloquent was the fact that they said nothing. They communicated by silence, until he closed the door and went back downstairs, sighing. After that, she slept. She must have been very tired, which would account for things being left off the table too.

Only illness could account for her being tired again this morning. In the kitchen, she wanted to sob over the fact that she was dying and there was no one to care. What vacancy would she leave? A bridge fourth could easily be found. And Dean would marry someone beautiful and younger, who knew how to play tennis, and Cynthia would have a companion. She regretted never having taken up tennis, as Dean and Cynthia had urged her to do. Sometimes on autumn or spring days, she felt stupid and logy indoors at a card table. Closely now, she often inspected the faces of other women her age, to see if she was aging more rapidly. But it was too late: she had no energy to run about a tennis court now. It was all she could do to swim a lap in a pool.

She made for breakfast a special favorite of Cynthia's, an omelet with freshly grated Parmesan. But Cynthia ate not only without thanks but without words of any kind. Her eyes were lowered, as if she were embarrassed about something, and taking her books, she left without good-bye.

The bridge club would look about the house; but if it was not spotless today, she could not help it. With her head aching, she could do little more than put fresh guest towels in the bathroom. Her headache began after Dean and Cynthia left. She sat at the table a long time, her head in her hands, and did not remember when Peter left, only that she told him he would have to find his boots alone, and to hurry.

How long ago it seemed that Dean teased her about the bridge club! The Lettuce-Leaf Club, he called it, and it was true that they ate little and concentrated mostly on frothy things to drink. She liked sweet drinks then, not being used to drinking. Now she would fix only things that tasted strongly of liquor, but the others had begun to object.

She had a special Bloody Mary recipe, calling for celery salt, and if she mixed a batch now, it would save time — although she promised herself, opening a can of tomato juice, she must not sample a drink. Other times, she had found that this was the danger of mixing drinks ahead. She stared in surprise at the bottle of vodka she had bought yesterday, now half empty. And a question throbbed dully, as faintly as her headache: Had she drunk that much alone?

To taste one Bloody Mary, after all, might help her headache: a thimbleful. She poured out a small amount of tomato-juice mixture, thoughtfully, and added an ounce of vodka to it.

With the guest towels in the bathroom, she looked about the house for any glaring disorder, then got out ice, with a feeling of triumph that she had met her deadline, after all. When the car turned into the driveway, she had another short

Bloody Mary, satisfying herself quickly that the cocktails had enough celery salt.

Mary Elena, leading the others into the house and bearing a platter of homemade candy, said, "You're looking happy for this time of morning."

"I had the most terrible headache," Ruth said, "and it's suddenly just gone. Your candy looks delicious and fattening. I think I'll try it after lunch."

Mary Elena urged candy on the others, but they declined too. She herself ate several pieces while Ruth stood holding the platter. For Ruth, too many things seemed to be happening at once, and she felt confused. Should she put the candy in the living room now, and would she remember to return the platter, and was the coffeepot ready to be plugged in? And here her guests stood, still crowded into the hall, waiting to be told to take off their coats. She held the dish tightly, telling them to go to her bedroom and knowing she needed a quiet drink before trying to put lunch on the table.

Chatting, removing coats, the women went upstairs while Ruth went into a kitchen that, suddenly confronting her with closed cabinets, was as inexplicable as someone else's kitchen. Where were things kept? At last she dumped the candy onto a counter top and took Mary Elena's platter to the hall table. From upstairs, Didi's rather dry voice said, ". . . again before we even got here," and she felt contented, glowing, thinking they spoke of her having things ready. Instead, Madge said, "If she can't keep her mind on the cards again today, I'm through," and Ruth moved swiftly away as they came down to the living room and Didi called, "Yoo-hoo, can we help?"

"I'm organized," she called back, keeping her voice steady and asking herself how she could be furious when she did not have the faintest idea what they were talking about. She doubted that they themselves knew. She poured drinks and drank part of hers and filled the glass again. She walked carefully into the living room and set down the tray, feeling them watch, and she smiled at them beautifully, knowing herself to be slightly bored by their conversation. She had entered to hear Mary Elena telling about something she had cooked that was good, and now Madge told of a new cake, with instant pudding inside, which they ought to try.

Why didn't they realize, she wondered, handing them drinks, how seldom she spoke of inconsequential things like recipes? Her thoughts were deeper than anyone realized. These women were never going to do anything, while she had a great long list of things she was going to do. They even drank ploddingly, which annoyed her. She had almost finished her drink and they were still sipping at theirs. Repeatedly, Mary Elena ate almonds from a dish everyone else avoided. Ruth smiled into her glass, watching; it seemed funny that Mary Elena was so fat she was fuzzy around the edges; against the room's plain wall, she was only an indistinguishable mound of something. Turning, Ruth stared out the window, and her thoughts drifted until she knew quite well that someday she was going to be a champion tennis player. Taking up tennis, quickly becoming a champion, she would show them all . . .

No one else wanted a second drink, and they went to the table while she took the tray to the kitchen. It seemed a shame to waste what was left in the pitcher, and lifting it, she drank. Amid a perplexing amount of dishes and candy scattered on a counter top, she found space to unmold the salad. It turned out well, and when she took it to the table, everyone exclaimed. "Madge, you start," she said, seeing that Madge had the serving pieces, and it seemed a moment of true inspiration when Ruth noticed the mayonnaise dish was still empty.

After replacing it on the table, filled, she sank into her own place, and felt heavy-eyed and sleepy. She was not hungry and ate little and did not join the conversation, mumbled around her as if she were underwater and the others above. With an elbow propped on the table, she slumped against one hand, wanting to put her head down. Her eyes forced open, she saw, in the middle of the table, the salad, forlorn-looking among a lot of lettuce.

"I forgot the cottage cheese!" she said, jumping up and hurrying the salad into the kitchen. There, the great pendulum of depression swung inside her again, and she wanted to weep, for the salad had not been glorious, after all. It had been a failure, like her life. What was she accomplishing standing here trying to mound cottage cheese into a gelatin ring with only two sides left to hold it? Tears did come, and she looked in despair at the four cocktail glasses. To put her head down and sob mournfully over all things gone wrong seemed her only hope. If she had not left college to marry, or had not married Dean, or had not married at all, and had not had a baby the first year, or had gone to secretarial school, or had been a nurse — wouldn't her life have gone somewhere?

Composed, she returned with the cottage cheese and urged it on everyone, suddenly longing for the women to be her friends, as if they were not. Wouldn't they tell her how they managed to sit here, the day beautiful and tiny birds hopping in the snow, without longing to drink all the dregs in the glasses in the kitchen? She went to make coffee and had to pass by the glasses again and ached with longing, as a tired person aches for sleep. She felt nothing from the drinks she had had; all she needed was a tiny bit more to make everything all right.

The women insisted she have two cups of coffee, to help her wake up, and Madge even carried a third cup for her to the bridge table. Her headache had come back, Ruth said, but she would play as long as possible. She could not manage those dishes on the table; Cynthia would have to do them when she came home. With dread, she thought of the evening; for once, Dean had said he would be home. But she would not be able to cook. He simply had to understand about the headaches that overtook her late in the afternoon. When he came home and found her in bed, he was always outraged, as if he had never expected her to have a headache again.

And then she saw from Madge's face, as she put down her cards, that she should not have raised Madge's bid. Excused, Ruth went to the bathroom and, with astonishment, saw that her face was bright red. Had she a fever? A cool cloth helped to subdue the flush slightly. Returning, she found that the others had decided to quit early, and she was grateful, though now that they were going, she felt lonely, and sorry for the things she had thought about them and hoped she had not said. She clung to Madge, apologizing over and over for raising the bid when she should not have, and for the rubber when she failed to trump, and for forgetting the cottage cheese and ruining the lunch. They all said, of course, that did not spoil lunch, it had been delicious, and Madge, untangling herself, said she was not sure she could play next week.

Then the house was melancholy with the leftover smells of their perfumes and cigarettes, and they seemed to have gone away in a huddled threesome to which she did not belong. Her third cup of coffee, still full, she carried to the sink to empty, and since there was no one to care whether she struggled and won or lost, and since it would serve Dean right, she poured what was left in the cocktail glasses into one glass and drank.

Whatever hour it was, the day was growing dark and it was beginning to snow. She undressed as far as her slip and sank onto the bed, pulling a comforter over her, knowing she was doing the only thing possible for a headache. Her charm bracelet caught on the coverlet, and she went to sleep thinking about untangling it later, when she woke.

Then she dreamed about the bracelet, that she had lost it, and every person she went to asking for it had just given it to someone else; and at last she cried in her sleep, "But don't you realize how much I've lost, that the charms are everything?"

She heard Cynthia and hoped she had the bracelet. Instead, Cynthia tugged at the covers, saying, "Mother, where's Peter?"

She sat up, and in the dressing-table mirror saw a woman in a disarranged satin slip, with tousled hair and swollen eyes. What day, what time was it? She had overslept and would be late getting breakfast again.

"Mother, where is Peter?" Cynthia said.

"Isn't he in bed? Have you waked him?"

Then Cynthia screamed, "It's almost seven at night! Is he at someone's house?"

Untangling the bracelet, Ruth stood unsteadily. Cold swept along the floor and covered her bare feet. She thought of the hour she had gone to bed; it was then that Peter should have come home. There was nothing to say but the truth: "I don't know where he is."

Thinking of Peter in the snow, she realized he was still almost a baby. Why hadn't she realized before? The night was enormous and dark, cold and snowing.

Cynthia — her child, too — had tears running down her face. "Mother, how could you not have watched Peter?" she said.

Dressed, Ruth went downstairs, her shoes in one hand, holding the banister with the other. In the hall, she put on her shoes, thinking she would have to call the police, and in that moment saw what they would see, coming in. There was the table full of dirty dishes, the salad dissolved, a cat eating the cottage cheese. The kitchen smelled of liquor, and there stood the empty vodka bottle and the four drained glasses. In a house where children lived and a husband was soon due, no one had started dinner. It struck her enormously that she was responsible for Peter's life. If he had been killed, hurt, maimed, frozen, no one should ever forgive her. No excuse would ever do.

"What are you going to do?" Cynthia asked.

"I'll have to call the police," she said, her hand on the phone. But at that instant, it rang, and a neighbor spoke, her voice distant, reserved, saying she had seen Peter out in the cold, without his boots, and had brought him inside, thinking surely Mrs. Parker would be home soon.

She motioned with a finger point for Cynthia to put on her coat and whispered where Peter was. Tears were in her eyes, and Cynthia, holding her boots, hesitated, then hugged her in relief. "My daughter's coming right over," she said, her voice clearing of its final thickness. She apologized, but realized from the silence at the other end of the phone that she could not win back Mrs. Goodwin, who, from observation, had formed an opinion of Peter's mother. But those close to her would see her change, she thought.

When Cynthia came back with Peter, the dishwasher had been emptied and loaded with the lunch dishes. Peter, hugged, was sent to have a warm bath and was promised fried chicken for dinner. He had come home, he said, and not finding anyone, had gone out to play and stayed a long time at Mrs. Goodwin's, waiting for lights to come on at his house.

"I'm sorry, Peter," she said, and looked at Cynthia. "The house won't be dark again when it shouldn't be."

Then, as Ruth watched him ascend the stairs, her headache

came back. Her hands shook as she bent to take chicken from the refrigerator, and she remained, her face thrust toward the coolness. She drew back, trying not to stare at the tomato juice; one quick drink would make her feel so much better. Tomorrow, a new day, she would begin over again. Why couldn't she forget about having a drink? Flouring the chicken, putting it on to fry, she could think only how good a drink would taste; when she felt sick like this, nothing else would help, though she was sorry.

Cynthia, coming in, glanced at her quickly, as if not looking.

Standing aside, Ruth said, "I'm having some of Mary Elena's candy. Want some?"

"What a bad example, before dinner," Cynthia said.

"Better than others," she said, and held out a piece to Cynthia, who took it slowly, as if understanding.

"It's good," Cynthia said, and watched her mother eat more.

But even when Cynthia had gone — and from the pencil-thin light in the hallway, she realized Cynthia had not completely closed her door — she felt sick from the smells of frying and grease and shut her eyes. In the room that seemed to move, she stood as if sleeping, and remembered her dream. She saw distinctly several dangling charms: two baby shoes; a house; a tree (to symbolize the first they owned, when they bought the house); a miniature wedding ring; a cat (now full of cottage cheese); a tiny pack of cards . . . And suddenly she understood the bereft mood of her dream: to lose the bracelet did mean losing everything, as Dean had warned her she would do.

Presently he opened the front door, looking apprehensively into his own house. In the kitchen, she faced him without speaking. His briefcase set down, he stared back as if at a stranger in his kitchen and said, "Didn't you have your bridge club today?"

She nodded, wishing he would not keep the distance of bright linoleum between them. She wondered how to tell what had happened without revealing exactly her part; but that was escape too, and she said, "I drank too much and went to sleep," hesitantly; but his eyes widened in perception. "And Peter got lost, but we found him. I don't want it to happen again."

"You want to stop drinking?"

"Yes, but I can't."

"How do you know that?"

"Because if you weren't here, I'd have a drink now."

Crossing the room, he put his arms about her; but love could not restrain her tomorrow, and she thought, how awful that something else could be stronger.

Dean said they would find help, and she went on cooking while he washed his hands. In other rooms, she heard the children moving about, getting ready for supper. To make life exciting, she had escaped it altogether. But now she had accepted its hardest lesson: It was ordinary, and this moment held no more than putting a platter of food on the table. Tomorrow at this time, the moment would be repeated.

Yet it was nice that the chicken smelled good and that people, hungry, were coming to eat. She heard their footsteps in the hall.

Against the windows the snow was turning to rain; hitting, it melted in slow drops. Wind bent branches that scraped the house. She was glad to be indoors and thought of the tiny birds she had seen that morning, pecking hopefully in the sun-bright snow. Now, somewhere out there, they were huddled against the night's buffeting wind. Leaning forward, she pressed her face in sympathy against the cold pane and thought, how incredible they survive, when there's so much to keep them from it.

Spring Is Now

ANDRA heard first in Miss Loma's store about the Negroes. She was buying cornstarch for her mother when Mr. Mal Walker rushed in, leaving his car at the gas pump, without filling it, to tell the news. His hair plastered to his forehead, he was as breathless and hot as if he had been running. "The school bus was loaded and the driver passed up some niggers in De Soto," he said. "They threw rocks at the bus and a brick that broke the driver's arm." That was all he knew about that. "But," he said, pausing until everyone in the store was paying attention. "There's some registered for your high school in Indian Hill."

At that moment Sandra found the cornstarch. The thought of going to school with Negroes leapt at her as confusedly as the box's yellow-and-blue design. Coming slowly around the bread rack, she saw Mal Walker, rapidly swallowing a Dr Pepper he had taken from the cold-drink case. She put the cornstarch on the counter. Miss Loma fitted a sack over the box and said, "Is that all?"

Sandra nodded and signed the credit pad Miss Loma shoved along the counter. In Miss Loma's pierced ears, small gold hoops shook as, turning back to Mal Walker, she said, "How many?"

"Three I heard." Almost smiling, he looked around and announced — as if the store were full of people, though there was only an apologetic-looking country woman, with a dime, waiting for the party line to clear — "If your kids haven't eat with niggers yet, they will have by Friday. I thank the Lord I live in Indian Hill. Mine will walk home to lunch. When it comes to eating with them, I draw the line."

"Sandra, you want something else?" Miss Loma said.

"No ma'am." Sandra went out and slowly up the hill toward her house opposite, thinking how many times she had eaten with Minnie, who worked for her mother, and how often her mother had eaten in the kitchen, while Minnie ironed. Even Grandmomma had said she would sit down with Minnie, Minnie was like one of the family, though Sandra could not remember that her grandmother ever had. For one reason, she was always in the living room looking at television. There now, she was shelling butter beans and Sandra passed behind her chair, saying nothing, because Grandmomma was hard of hearing. In the kitchen, Sandra put down the cornstarch and said, "Mother, Mister Mal Walker says there's Negroes coming to our high school."

"Are you sure?" Her mother, Flo, was frying chicken and stood suddenly motionless, a long-handled fork outstretched over the skillet full of popping meat and grease. She and Sandra had similar pale faces and placid gray-green eyes, which they widened now, in worry. "I guess we knew it was coming," Flo said.

"Three, he thinks."

In bifocals, Grandmomma's eyes looked enormous. She stood in the doorway saying, "Three what?" Having seen Flo motionless, she sensed something had happened and hearing what, she threw her hands to her throat and said, "Oh, you don't mean to tell me." With the fork, Flo stuck chicken pieces,

[114]

lifting them onto paper toweling. "Now, Momma," she said, "we knew it was coming." Then Grandmomma, resigned to one more thing she had not expected to live to see, let her hands fall to her sides. "I sure do hate to hear it," she said. "Are they girls and boys?"

"I don't know," Sandra said.

"I just hope to goodness it's girls," Grandmomma said, looking at Flo, who said again, "Now, Momma."

At sundown, when her father came from the fields, Sandra was watching television with Grandmomma. The pickup stopped, a door slammed, but the motor continued to run. From the window she saw her father, a sturdy, graying man; he was talking to Willson, a field hand, who backed the truck from the drive as her father came inside. "Daddy," she said, "there's Negroes going to our school."

He stood a moment looking tired from more than work. Then he said, "I guess it had to happen." He frowned and his eyebrows drew together across his forehead. "The schools that don't take them don't get government money. I knew you'd be with them at the university. But I'm sorry you had to start a year earlier."

Grandmomma, looking up from her program, said, "I just hope they're girls."

"Oh, Grandmomma," Sandra said with irritation and followed her father across the hall. "Why'd Willson take the truck, Daddy?"

Having bent over the bathroom basin to wash, he lifted his head. "That boy of his sick in Memphis can come home tonight. I loaned him the truck to go get him," he said, and his splashed face seemed weighted by the drops of water falling away.

"The one that's had all that trouble with his leg swelling?" Flo said. She brought the platter of chicken to the table.

"He's on crutches but will be all right," the father said.

"I declare, that boy's had a time," Grandmomma said, joining them at the table. "When Willson brings the truck, give him some of my grape jelly to carry to the boy."

They bent their heads and Sandra's father said his usual long blessing. Afterward they looked at one another across the centerpiece of zinnias, as if words were left unsaid. But no one said anything and they began to eat. Then the father said, "Guess what happened? Willson and some of his friends asked if I'd run for road supervisor."

"Why, Tate," Flo said. "What'd you say?"

"I said, 'When would I find the time?' " he said.

"It shows the way they're thinking." Flo said.

"How?" Sandra said.

"They know they can't run one of them yet, but they want a man elected they choose," she said. "Still, Tate, it's a compliment."

"I guess it is," he said.

"The time's just going to come," Grandmomma said.

"Of course, it is," he said.

At six-fifteen the next morning, Sandra from her bed heard a repeated knock rattling the side door. There were the smells of coffee and sausage, and Flo, summoned, pushed her chair from the table to answer the door. Air-conditioning so early made the house too cold and Sandra, reaching for her thin blanket, kept her eyes closed.

"Morning, how're you?" It was Johnson, the Negro who cleaned the Methodist church. He had come to get his pay from Flo, the church's treasurer.

"Pretty good, Johnson, how're you?" Flo said.

"Good but not pretty." He and Flo laughed, then were quiet while she wrote the check. Sandra heard him walk off down the gravel drive and it seemed a long time before she fell back to sleep. Then Flo shook her, saying, "Louise wants to drive the car pool today. You have to be at school at ten to register. Hurry, it's after nine."

"Why'd Johnson come so early?" she said.

"Breakfast was the only time he knew he could catch me home," Flo said.

Drinking orange juice, Sandra stood by the refrigerator and Grandmomma called from the living room, "Are you going to school all winter with your hair streaming down your back like that? I wish you'd get it cut today."

"I don't want it cut," Sandra said.

"Well, I wish you'd wear it pretty like this girl on television then. Look, with it held back behind a band like that."

Sandra came into the living room to look. "Her hair's in a pageboy; it's shorter than mine," she said.

"At least comb it," her mother called from the kitchen.

"I combed it!" Sandra said.

"Well you need to comb it again," her mother said. "And eat something."

"I'm not hungry in the mornings," Sandra said and went out into the heat and down the steep driveway to wait for her friend Louise. There was no high school in their town and they went twenty miles away to a larger place. "Cold," Sandra said, getting in Louise's car.

"Turn that valve and the air conditioner won't blow straight on you," Louise said. She pushed back hair that fell, like a mane, over her glasses. "You heard?"

"About the Negroes?"

"Yes. I heard there were thirteen."

"Thirteen! I heard three."

Louise laughed. "Maybe there's none and everybody's excited about nothing."

There had been a drought all summer in northwest Mississippi. They rode looking out at cotton fields nowhere near bloom, corn limp and brown, and soybeans stunted, flat to the ground. Between the fields were stretches of crumbly dirt, enormous and empty, where crops failed from the drought had been plowed under. Nearby, a pickup raced along a gravel road and as far as they could see, dust trailed it, one cloud rising above the flatland. Once, workmen along the road turned to them faces yellowed by dust, with dark holes for eyes, and Sandra thought of the worry that had been on her father's face all summer, as farmers waited for rain. And all summer, wherever they went, her mother had said, "You don't remember what it was like before everybody had air-conditioned cars. All this dust blew in the windows. Whew! I don't know how we stood it."

And, not remembering she had said it before, Grandmomma would say, "You don't remember either what it was like trying to sleep. Sometimes we'd move our mattresses out into the yard and sleep under the trees. We'd wring out towels and put them on the bed wet to cool the sheets." That she had lived then, though she did not remember it, seemed strange to Sandra.

At school, she found out only that some Negroes had already registered. None were there and the teachers would answer no other questions. Standing in long lines all morning, Sandra found she watched for the Negroes anyway. Other students said they had done the same. She thought the Negroes had been paid more attention by being absent than if they had been present. On the way home, Louise said, "If it weren't such a mystery, I don't think I'd think much about them. If there's a few, I just feel I'm not going to bother them and they're not going to bother me, if they're not smart-alecky."

[118]

"I know," Sandra said. "What's the difference, three or thirteen, with the rest of us white?" They stopped on the highway at the Mug'n Cone for hot dogs and root beer. Nearing home, Sandra began to dread questions she would be asked, particularly since she knew little more than when she left. At Miss Loma's, she got out to buy shampoo. The old men were gathered on the store porch playing dominoes, and she said only, "Afternoon," though her mother always said they would be glad for conversation. She thought of when her grandfather had been among them and entered the store.

Miss Loma had already heard the news from the Indian Hill school. She and a Memphis salesman were talking about a family nearby, in the Delta, who passed as white, though people steered clear of them, believing they had Negro blood. "I'll tell you how you can always tell a Negro," the salesman said. "By the blue moons on their nails. They can't hide those."

"I've heard," Miss Loma said, her earrings shaking, "they have black streaks at the ends of their spinal cords. Now, that's what men who've been with them in the army say. Of course, I don't know if it's true. I doubt it." She and the salesman could not decide whether she ought to stock up on straight-lined or dotted-lined primary tablets. With a practical finger, Miss Loma twirled the wire school-supply rack. The salesman pushed back a sporty straw hat with a fishing-fly ornament and said, "Wait till school starts and see what the teacher wants. One thing I hate to see is, somebody stuck with primary tablets they can't sell."

An amber container decided Sandra on a shampoo. She brought the bottle to the counter. "I've heard," she said, "they wear makeup on TV that'll make them look whiter."

"Of course they do," Miss Loma said.

Also, Sandra had heard that Negroes never kissed one another. They made love without preliminaries, like animals, or did nothing. But she was afraid to offer that information. Sometimes, even her mother and father did not seem to know she knew people made love.

Miss Loma said, "Honey, take that shampoo on home as a present. Happy birthday."

"How'd you know it was my birthday?"

"A bird told me."

"Grandmomma," Sandra said.

"You heard about the little nigger baby up in Memphis that's two parts animal?" the salesman said.

"No!" Miss Loma said.

"It's got a little dear face and bare feet," the salesman said, and when Sandra went out, he and Miss Loma were laughing.

In his dusty, green pickup, Sandra's father drew up to the gas pump. Willson's wife, along with another Negro woman, stepped from the truck's cab and went into a grocery across the road. "I see you got your nigger women with you today, Tate," said one of the old men playing dominoes.

Lifting the hose, Sandra's father stood putting in gas, laughing. "Yeah, I carried them with me today," he said. "Sandra, I got to go on back to the field. There's a dressed chicken on the front seat Ida sent. Take it on to your Momma." Sandra opened the truck's door, thinking how many people made remarks about her father letting Negroes ride up front with him. He always answered that if somebody asked him for a ride, he gave it to them; why should they sit out in the open truck bed covered with dust and hit by gravel? She heard him call into the store, "Four-ninety for gas, Loma," and holding the chicken, Sandra waved as he drove off.

Ida's husband had been a field hand for Sandra's father and now was too old to work. Sandra's father let the old couple stay on, rent free, in the cabin on his land. Ida raised chickens and brought one to Flo whenever she killed them. When Flo went to the bakery in Indian Hill, she brought Ida something sweet. Sandra came into the kitchen now and put the chicken on the sink. "That's a nice plump one," Flo said. "If we hadn't had chicken last night, I'd put it on to cook. I hope your daddy let Ida know how much we appreciate it."

"He says he always thanks her," Sandra said.

"But I don't know whether he thanks her enough," her mother said.

The kitchen smelled of cake baking and Sandra pretended not to notice. "Aren't you going to ask about the Negroes at school?" she said.

"Honey, I couldn't wait for you to come wandering in. I called around till I found out."

"I don't see why they got to register at a special time. Why couldn't they register when we did?" Sandra said.

"I don't understand it myself," Flo said.

"I don't understand why they have to be there at all," Grandmomma said, on her way to the bathroom during a commercial. "I declare, I don't."

"Oh Grandmomma," Sandra said.

"I guess they didn't want to take chances on trouble during registration," Flo said. "If the Negroes are just there when school starts, no one can say anything."

"There's plenty of things folks could say if they just would," Grandmomma called.

"I thought she was hard of hearing," Sandra said.

"Not all of the time," Flo said. When Grandmomma came back through the kitchen, Flo said, "We haven't had anything to say about what's happened so far. Everything else has just been shoved down our throats, Mother. I don't know why you think we'd have a chance to say anything now." Sandra, going out and down the hall, wondered why her mother bothered trying to explain to Grandmomma. "What are you going to do?" Flo called.

"Wash my hair," Sandra said.

"Well, for heaven's sake, roll it up as tight as you can and try to keep it curled."

"I wish you'd put it behind a band like that girl on television," Grandmomma called, and Sandra closed the bathroom door.

The candles flickered, then burned, as Flo hesitated in the doorway, smiling, before bringing the decorated cake in to supper. The family sang "Happy Birthday" to Sandra. Her father rolled in a portable television atop brass legs and she jumped up with a squeal. Her hair, waved and tied with a ribbon to please them, loosened and fell toward her shoulders. Now she could see programs without arguing with Grandmomma.

Flo's face was in wrinkles, anxious, as though she feared Ida had not been thanked enough for a chicken, and Sandra knew she was to like her grandmomma's present more than ordinarily. On pink tissue paper, in a tiny box, lay a heavy gold pin twisted like rope into a circle. "Why, Grandmomma!" Sandra said in surprise. Her exclamation was taken for admiration and everyone looked pleased. When she had gone into Grandmomma's room as a small child, to poke among her things, she had been shown the pin. Grandmomma's only heirloom, it had been her own mother's. "I've been afraid I wouldn't live till you were sixteen," Grandmomma said. "But I wanted to give you the pin when you were old enough to appreciate it."

"She never would give it even to me," Flo said.

"No, it was to be for my first grandchild," Grandmomma said. "I decided that when Momma died and left it to me. It was all in the world she had to leave and it's all I've got. But I want you to enjoy it now, instead of when I'm gone."

Had she made enough fuss over the pin? Sandra asked later. Flo said she had, but to thank her grandmother occasionally again. "Mother, it's not really the kind of pin anyone wears," Sandra said. The pin hung limply, lopsided, on her striped turtleneck jersey.

Flo said, "It is kind of heavy and antique. Maybe you'll like it when you're grown. Wear it a few times anyway."

The morning that school started, Sandra hung the pin on her coat lapel and forgot it. She walked into her class and there sat a Negro boy. His simply sitting there was disappointing; she felt like a child who had waited so long for Christmas that when it came, it had to be a letdown. He was to be the only Negro in school. The others had changed their minds, the students heard. But by then everyone had heard so many rumors, no one knew what to believe. The Negro was tall and light-skinned. Louise said the officials always tried to send light-skinned ones first. He was noticeably quiet and the girls, at lunch, found he had spoken in none of his classes. Everyone wondered if he was smart enough to be in the school. From her table Sandra saw him eating by a window with several other boys. Still, he seemed alone and she felt sorry for him.

In the car pool with her and Louise were two boys, Don and Mark. Don, the younger, was an athlete. Going home that afternoon, he said the Negro was not the type for football but was so tall, maybe he would be good at basketball. Sandra thought how little she knew about the Negro and how many questions she would be asked. He had worn a blue shirt, she remembered, and he was thin. Certainly, he was clean. Grandmomma would ask that. She did not even know the Negro's name until Don said, "He lives off this road."

"Who?" she said.

"The colored boy, Jack Lawrence," he said.

"We could ask him to be in the car pool," Louise said, laughing.

Mark, sandy-haired and serious, said, "You all better watch your talk. I had my interview at the university this summer and ate lunch in the cafeteria. There were lots of Negroes and all kinds of people. Indians. Not with feathers, from India. Exchange students."

Dust drifted like clouds over fields, and kudzu vine, taking over the countryside, filling ditches and climbing trees, was yellowed by it. Young pines, set out along the road banks, shone beneath a sun that was strong, even going down. Sandra looked out at tiny pink flowers just appearing on the cotton and tried to imagine going as far away, to a place as strange, as India. That Indians had come all the way to Mississippi to school made her think about people's lives in a way she never had. She entered the house saying, before Grandmomma could ask questions, "Grandmomma, you know they got Indians from India going to Ole Miss?"

Grandmomma looked up through the lower half of her glasses. "You don't mean to tell me," she said, and it took away some of her curiosity about the Negro too. At supper, Sandra gave all the information she could. The Negro boy was clean, looked nice, and his name was Jack Lawrence. All the information she could give in the next month was that he went his way and she went hers. Finally even Grandmomma stopped asking questions about him. He and Sandra had no reason to speak until one morning, she was working the combination to her locker when a voice, quite deep, said, "Sandra, you left this under your desk."

Her dark hair fell forward. In the moment that she pushed it back, something in the voice's deep tone made her think unaccountably how soft her own hair felt. Jack Lawrence held out the book she had forgotten, his face expressionless. It would have been much more natural for him to smile. She saw for the first time how carefully impersonal he was. Other students had mentioned that he never spoke, even to teachers, unless spoken to first. She smiled and said, "Lord, math. I'm bad enough without losing the book too. Thanks."

"Okay. I just happened to notice you left it." He started down the hall and Sandra joined him, as she would have anyone going the way she was. She held her books against her, as if hugging herself in anticipation, but of what, she did not know. She had a curiously excited feeling to be walking beside anyone so tall. No, she thought, not anyone, a boy. They talked about the afternoon's football game, then Jack Lawrence continued down the hall and Sandra turned into her class. There was certainly nothing to that, she thought. But Louise, leaning from her desk, whispered, "What were you talking *about?*"

"Football," Sandra said, shrugging. She thought of all the Negroes she had talked to in her life, of those she talked to every day, and wondered why it was strange to talk to Jack Lawrence. Her mother complained that at every meal, Sandra's father had to leave the table, answer the door, and talk to some Negro who worked for him. They would stand together a long time, like any two men, her father propping his foot on the truck's bumper, smoking and talking. Now she wondered what they talked about.

Jack Lawrence's eyes, when she looked into them, had been brown. Were the eyes of all Negroes? From now on, she would notice. On her way to the stadium that afternoon, she wondered if her gaiety was over the football game or the possibility of seeing — not the Negro, she thought, but Jack Lawrence? Louise went ahead of her up the steps and turned into the bleachers. "I have to sit higher," Sandra said, "or I can't see," adding, "Lon's up there." Louise was crazy about Lon, the basketball coach's son, and rising obediently, she followed Sandra to a seat below him. Lon was sitting with Jack Lawrence. Looking up, Sandra smiled but Jack Lawrence turned his eyes to the game and his lips made no movement at all. When she stood to cheer, to buy a Coke, popcorn, a hot dog, Sandra wondered if he watched her. After the game, he and Lon leapt from the bleachers and went out a back way. That night, she slept with a sense of disappointment.

At school, she always nodded and spoke to him and he spoke back: but they did not walk together again. Most often, he was alone. Even to football games, he did not bring a friend. There was a Thanksgiving dance in the gym, festooned with balloons and crepe paper, but he did not come. On Wednesday before the holiday, driving the car pool, Sandra had seen Jack Lawrence walking along a stretch of country road, hunched into his coat. The motor throbbed loudly in the cold country stillness as she stopped the car and said, "You want a ride?"

He stood, looking as if he did not want any favors, but with eyes almost sore-looking from the cold, then climbed into the back seat with Don and Mark. The countryside's stillness came again as Sandra stopped at the side road he mentioned. With coat collar turned up, untangling long legs, he got out. She was aware of the way her hair hung, of her grandmother's pin too old and heavy for her coat, of the skirt that did not cover her knees, which Grandmomma said was indecent. And she was aware of him, standing in the road

[126]

against the melancholy winter sunset, looking down to say, "Thank you."

"You're welcome," she said, looking up.

That night she asked her father whether she should have given Jack Lawrence a ride. Her father said she was not to give a ride to Negroes when she was alone. "Not even to women?" she said.

"Oh well, to women," he said.

"Not even to Willson?" she said.

Her father seemed to look inward to himself a long time, then he answered, "No, not even to Willson."

Thanksgiving gave Sandra an excuse to start a conversation. She saw Jack Lawrence in the hall the first day afterward and said, "Did you have a nice holiday?"

"Yes," he said. "Did you?"

Sandra mentioned, briefly, things she had done. "Listen," she said. "We go your way every day, if you'd like a ride."

"Thanks," he said, "but most of the time I have one." He turned to his locker and put away his books and Sandra, going on down the hall, had the strangest feeling that he knew something she did not. She remained friendly, smiling when she saw him, though he made no attempt to talk. He only nodded and smiled when they met and she thought he seemed hesitant about doing that. She asked the boys in the car pool questions about him. Why hadn't he gone out for basketball, how were his grades, what did he talk about at lunch, did anybody know exactly where he lived, besides down that side road? — until one day, Louise said, "Sandra, you talk about that Negro so much, I think you like him."

"Yes, I like him. I mean, I don't dislike him, do you? What reason would we have."

"No, I don't dislike him," Louise said. "He's not at all smart-alecky."

In winter when they came home from school, it was dark. Flo said, "If you didn't have those boys in your car pool, I'd drive you girls back and forth myself. I don't know what Don and Mark could do if anything happened, but I feel better they're there." Sandra's parents, everyone, lived in fear of something happening. South of them, in the Delta, there was demonstrating, and Negroes tried to integrate restaurants and movies in several larger towns. Friends of Sandra's mother began carrying tear gas and pistols in their pocketbooks. Repeatedly, at the dinner table, in Miss Loma's, Sandra heard grown-ups say, "It's going to get worse before it gets any better. We won't see the end of this in our lifetime." Grandmomma always added, "I just hate to think what Sandra and her children will live to see."

One day after Christmas vacation, those in the car pool again saw Jack Lawrence walking along the road. "Should we stop?" Louise said. She was driving, with Don beside her.

"Of course. Would you just drive past him?" Sandra said. She was sitting in the back seat with Mark, and when Jack Lawrence climbed into the car, she was sitting between them. They spoke of the cold, of the snow that had fallen after Christmas, the deepest they could ever remember, and of how you came across patches of it, still, in unexpected places. Side roads were full of frozen ruts. Jack Lawrence said he hated to think of the mud when a thaw came. There could be one at any time. That was the way their weather was. In the midst of winter, you could suddenly have a stretch of bright, warm, almost spring days. There was a silence and Jack Lawrence, looking down at Sandra, said, "Did you lose that pin you always wear?"

"Oh Lord," Sandra said, her hand going quickly, flat, against her lapel.

"Sandra, your Grandmomma's pin!" Louise said, looking into the rearview mirror.

"Maybe it fell off in the car," Mark said. The three in back put their hands down the cracks around the seat. Sandra felt in her pockets, shook out her skirt. They held their feet up and looked under them. Don, turning, said, "Look up under the front seat."

Bending forward at the same instant, Sandra and Jack Lawrence knocked their heads together sharply. "Ow!" Mark cried out for them, while tears came to Sandra's eyes. They clutched their heads. Their faces were close, and though Sandra saw yellow, dancing dots, she thought, Of course Negroes kiss each other when they make love. She and Jack Lawrence fell back against the seat laughing, and seemed to laugh for miles, until she clutched her stomach in pain.

"Didn't it hurt? How can you laugh so?" Louise said.

"I got a hard head," Jack Lawrence said.

When he stood again in the road thanking them, his eyes, glancing into the car, held no message for Sandra. Tomorrow, he said silently, by ignoring her, they would smile and nod. That they had been for a time two people laughing together was enough. As they rode on, Sandra held tightly the pin he had found, remembering how she had looked at it one moment lying in his dark hand, with the lighter palm, and the next moment, she had touched the hand lightly, taking the pin. Opening her purse, she dropped the pin inside.

"Is the clasp broken?" Mark said.

"No, I guess I didn't have it fastened good," she said.

"Aren't you going to wear it anymore?" Louise said, looking back.

"No," she said.

"What will your grandmomma say?" Louise said.

"Nothing I can worry about," Sandra said.

[129]

Jesse

*H*E knew that he had been cheated. In an old green handbag of his wife's, hanging on the cabin wall, were the ten folded receipts of his sharecropping years. Often he took them out to look at again, but they remained inscrutable. The receipts were written on lined tablet paper, and their creases grown dirty were beginning to tear and the blue lines fading were whitened, like veins let with water. Into many dark nights he asked his question: "You know what sharecropping is?" And gave his own answer: "Big debts, slaving work, having to keep my chillen out of school and nothing to show for it at the end."

Night's only consolation was it blocked out sight of the kitchen's wood stove when he had promised May Dean an electric one; and night hid unpainted walls, unsettled floors, an old wringer washer and seven children in two beds in the cabin's other two rooms. But morning brought them to sight again, and nothing softened in the sun's first glow. Nothing sprang alive in its later gleam. Nothing at all sparkled in its midday strength. By late afternoon when the sun had gone, the cabin's dry cedarwood took on the colorless look of tears, and the broad sky, over fields, had the silver look of fish. But he came along the road then, too tired to notice.

His chillen never had had the right thing to wear to school. He said it aloud, sitting in one straight chair, while May Dean sat in the other. Endlessly, they talked or looked at one another without speaking, as if to do either thing would find an answer. May Dean always said, "I stood there and told that white man my chillen didn't have shoes and were cold; we were picking cotton in January that year." Jesse listened without growing tired of the story's repetition, the way some men grew tired of listening to their wives; one reason, he said, so many left out from home. Though the main reason was not being able to get enough food and clothes. Meeting every morning eight pairs of eyes across a table almost empty, with groceries natural-born high and even fatback seventy cents a pound, did something, inside deep, where he was supposed to feel safely a man.

May Dean would continue, "I carried the paper with me and ast Boss man, 'Explain.' I'd stand up there and argue and say what I understood and what I didn't; and he'd say not to worry, it was all right." Stubbornly hidden lay the answer to how you could work a year and end up owing money. Folded, unfolded, refolded, the receipts helped Jesse to go back over the years again. Otherwise, one year did not stand out from another, the way the children's births, coming so close, did not seem separate. Sunup to sundown, he had worked as sharecroppers do and, unrelievedly, there had been the fields and on their far edges, beyond reach when he came to the end of a hot row, trees and shade. The children he held in his mind as the oldest, the youngest, and the ones in the middle were simply his children. In the same way, he thought collectively of his crops, and only catastrophe, attaching itself to one or the other, made them stand out. One crop year, the second-youngest girl swelled all over from wasp bites; the middle boy caught his eyelid on a fishhook; and the

[134]

third girl had to be carried to the doctor three times another year, sick. Spring, a few years ago, in 1960, had been stormy and wild and they had waked to thunder, rain, and hail day after day; cotton already planted had to be replanted — and a third time some places; they had done the work without hope, knowing it would be a bad year, for June cotton, dogtail cotton, never brought a good price. After the long wetness, there had been a long dryness, and the June temperature stood at ninety. Dust had blown up from the sandy roads and covered everything, and Jesse, leaning on his hoe, could not help but envy its destination, which was anywhere, everywhere. May Dean, resting, had watched too and they had stared out of eyes dark and mournful as a skeleton's, set in faces grown ashy with the dust. Whitened, their shoes were lost in the field and their clothes were turned the color of the sun-streaked sky. Set out in a row behind them, like the plants themselves, the children stopped too; he saw them then; six, old enough to be worth three dollars a day, chopping.

The white man's crops suffered the same tornadoes and his cotton burned up under the same sun; he too had had to replant, and his bales brought the same price, which was why, taking down the green pocketbook, opening a receipt, Jesse did not understand. There were the figures for the total sale of cotton, for his half, with his furnish subtracted, and finally the amount he had earned.

"One hundred sixty-two dollars, and I worked a year," he said.

"And 'leven cents," May Dean added, knowing just which year he meant.

" 'Leven cents," he repeated. One cone of cream — for seven kids — and a penny left. Then in the room was only the frail sound of another receipt being opened. Things charged against him made certain years more vivid: seventy dollars for furniture the same year the girl had to be carried to the doctor three times. They had needed the third bed and needed another now and there was nothing he would not buy for May Dean if he could; he had been glad to get a kitchen table and a few other things she had wanted. Yet, having gotten them, the house still looked sorry; and he had been out the money too.

For the cabin, he paid seven dollars a month rent, but it did not seem worth that. He aimed for one of the Government houses in town, though the rent was three times as much. They had no car to get back and forth; but if they lived in town, the chillen could get little piddling jobs, cutting grass, deliverying, and May Dean could get a little piddling job and then they could make it; couldn't they?

He did not ask the question aloud, but in the other chair, gazing toward the road, May Dean seemed to know it. Dust, in summer, spewed from cars passing in the road close and from children playing in the dirt yard and kept her busy sweeping. In winter, ashes sifted from the wood settling in the stove as they slept and the walls all seasons held that sweet smoke smell, as the night held always his question.

Often he opened only the final receipt, faded too, though the scene it brought back was clear. In the white man's weighing station, he had stood, cap in his hand. A heater burned hot as mid-summer when sweat frazzled the cotton rows into a moving pattern, like water fleeing racing motorboats when he was trying to fish quietly at the Government dam. Sweating, he had seen the white man's eyes dilate and thought, He's thinking, nigger smell. And he had wanted to say, "White man, you ever tried bathing under a pump?" But what words had he known to prove the receipt wrong? He only repeated, "I made twenty bales of cotton."

And the white man, an equal number of times, replied, "I know, Jesse. But facts and figures speak for themselves. It's a bad year for everybody."

A bad year for one meant a bad year for all; Jesse knew that. But the facts and figures did not speak to that man what they spoke to him. An item read "Doctor For Wife," and he saw May Dean holding her stomach too soon for the last baby to come. Reading "Dentist," he remembered how long he had let the oldest boy suffer before carrying him there, having prayed the toothache would go away. And "Groceries" were the ones in the store they could not afford and the dollar they paid someone to carry them to the store and back. He stared at the orderly list: lights, plowing, poisoning, fertilizer, feed-sack bills. In the hot room with the heater he thought of the fields with his wife and children, out of school, chopping cotton; the long, hot, dusty autumn days and shade trees, tarnished like copper, ever out of reach on the edges of the fields; the cotton in bloom; and sacks on their backs heavier as the days grew heavier; at last, the bales stood bound with hoops untouchable in the sun. Sunup to sundown, until the work was done, and then, taking off his cap, he was standing where the blue leaping in the gas heater's jets was the same blue as the white man's eyes, hearing him say, "You come out owing me four hundred dollars this year, Jesse."

"But I made twenty bales of cotton."

Facts, figures, speak for themselves. A bad year for everybody.

He had thought, But your chillen'll have Christmas and your house is not a shack. Equally they had worked and the other had come out ahead. Always, everywhere, in places above him, boss man had won out. In control, he had thought. Black, white: they had shared equally and yet it was the white man saying, "Here, get those kids some Christmas," handing him two dollars, which he took, his pride being a lesser thing than his children having candy for Christmas.

Then night had been neither of the things it had been so long, a time for exhaustion or for love. Even after fifteen years, May Dean was always like a blossom beneath him, opening to him, as sweet as the pink bloom that came on cotton late in the season. She was younger and her face was smooth and gold as liquid honey; her teeth were small and even and when she smiled her cheeks rose and shone as if they had been polished. She laughed all the time, while he seldom did, and when he made promises she listened and believed. He was black and at forty-three it was with effort that his cheeks rose at all; instead the skin folded into long tired lines along his face; there were hollows beneath his eyes, which made them seem larger. They were round and very dark and his desire to accomplish stood out in them. That time, the night had been for moving. Stealthily, they went away from the place that had been home and could not look back. They had to leave the dog in its dug-out place beneath the front porch and some of the children cried. A man from their church had carried them in his pickup and charged only for the gas. People in nearby cabins heard and came and quietly and quickly their things were loaded. Then those people crept back home and tomorrow would say they knew nothing of the leaving of Jesse Barnes and his family. Only when they had gone too far to turn back did May Dean remember she had left clothes on the line. It took away from his total satisfaction in leaving the white man in debt.

They had lived with May Dean's brother in another town until Jesse found another job and this cabin. "I been a slave all my life, sharecropping," he told the brother-in-law. "It's the biggest trap you ever saw, I made a lot of money but I didn't get none of it. I didn't get nothing out of it."

Then they were in the fields again, the children out of school; the same as his own life had been, he thought, hoeing; just exactly the same thing. He had left school after fourth grade to help his Daddy; but how much time had he been in school when he was there: a piece of a year here and a piece there when it was not crop time, passed along from one grade to another, the way colored chillen had to be, without grades having any meaning at all. He had not known himself what grade he was in until he left school and they told him. Nothing had come of all the years afterward and the doors he had tried to open were still closed. Now he saw if he could spell and read better, he might have done better. He could figure some; write; but his spelling was another thing.

Then a law was passed the children could not be taken out of school to chop and he saw them individually: marching six strong from the field, only the baby left, napping in the shade out of the sun's reach. In the field alone, he and May Dean had to let go the garden they had managed without a mule, with not an hour of daylight left between them when they could care for it. Greens came up volunteer that spring and when they were eaten that was the garden's end. Untended, wire surrounding it came uprooted and slowly disappeared. "We could have sold that wire," May Dean said.

"I was going to," he said, "when I found time to roll it up." But he was glad about the children going to school all year. Other Negroes said things were better and better, but he saw nothing better about the price of groceries or a mule or the hour the sun rose and finally set. Maybe they meant better because of the civil-rights workers who came that summer, bringing hope at a time when he had just about given out of it. So tired had he been at night, lying flat and still, he seldom even thought of opening the blossom that was May Dean. As little education as he had, he could see farming was just about run out. It meant six months work and with prices the way they were, everybody needed a job that ran from year to year. Factories had come to many of the small towns and for Negroes qualified for jobs in those, things were better.

Better meant the arrival the second summer of the civil-rights workers, who mingled with Negroes as if they were people. He and May Dean made a particular friend named Charlie. Sunday afternoons, May Dean cooked a good country dinner and Charlie sat on the front porch asking him about himself in a way no one ever had. It was then he recalled being the little boy who had wanted to go to school and had to pick cotton instead. He laughed about the one-room school, remembering how cold his fingers and feet had been and how other times sweat, collecting from all over him, had run down his legs, soaking his pants as if through accident. His books had been raggedy, missing pages, and he had not minded until all these years later. Charlie, in his early twenties, peered through greenish glasses that seemed heavier than himself. He said in the fall he was going to Europe to study painting and, one Sunday, arriving with some rags and a flat brown case, he told Jesse he wanted to paint his cabin. "You going to paint all of it?" Jesse had said, and it was not until then Charlie realized he needed to explain further about his painting. It seemed an enormous thing for that boy to be going off across all that water alone. He and May Dean thought how far they had been, to Memphis and back. They asked if Charlie wasn't afraid and when he said no, Jesse tried to imagine belonging to the world he was afraid to turn his back on. He tried to imagine other places but in his mind never left home. Other possibilities escaped him. It took nearly the summer of

Sundays before Charlie could convince him to look for work off the farm. "You've said it's a way of life gone by. Now are you going to be left behind?" Charlie said.

May Dean, in a plum-purple skirt, sat pressing and pressing its pleats with fingers as padded and white on the insides as kitten's paws. For the first time, her eyes did not meet his. The question had been hesitant, testing; Jesse felt Charlie had looked at him as if through a screen door he was not sure could be pushed. That boy was frail as a whip but just as smart and more than twenty years younger, and the challenge that rose in Jesse had nothing at all to do with color. He felt himself pull himself up a long road — with a vision of himself very rich, like one of his own people on television, and going back and paying that man four hundred dollars — then he said, "I been thinking what to do. The highway's taking on people to lay pipes."

"Good, Jesse," Charlie said. "I'll take you over in my car to apply."

And May Dean grinned with her fine teeth, lighting up the soft places on her cheeks, and her fingers relaxed pressing her skirt as if maybe now she would have a new one. He became a commuter, a new word for him. But first he had to get to the highway, to the meeting place, where the job began. Down the road, a man said he would carry him and bring him home at night, for a dollar a day: which is what the others who rode with him paid; what choice did he have? Five dollars a week for four weeks a month almost ate up the profits of the new job. On trucks they went up and down the highway clear to Memphis, starting in the early morning when it was still cool, and they were back home, off work, before the stores closed in town. Never in his life had his working hours been controlled by the hands of a clock. The seasons had set his hours. The sun had made them long and the rain sometimes had made them short. He had never gone to work at exactly the same time but tarried at home or left the field early if he saw the need in clouds banked in an uncertain sky. He had taken off time to kill rabbits or to fish if they were biting. When the Fair came to Memphis, he and the family went whatever day they could catch a ride. He drew money if the weather was bad or he was sick. But the state paid for the exact number of hours he put in. The man with the car stopped beyond his house at a crossroads — where crumbling mud-banks were taller than his head and tree roots exposed were gaunt and gray, reaching toward the road like fumbling fingers; and if he was not already there, waiting, the man grew mad and blew his horn and threatened next time to leave him. "Jesse, you better get a run on," the driver would call.

"Cat, you better get used to being on time," a younger man said when he was late again, and Jesse felt shame, riding on in the car as if he had been running not to be on time but to catch up.

That winter, the trucks took him south and farther from home than he had ever wanted to be. Nights they stayed away lengthened into weeks and May Dean stayed on his mind, close to the road in the cabin that could barely withstand winter, much less a stranger wanting in. He felt no need to go out from camp, into town, as the young men did. Away from them, the children stood out in his mind. He wondered if John, the oldest, was doing his schoolwork and if Lu Ann, the oldest girl, was helping May Dean with the wash and the baby, and if all were walking safely in the road, far to one side. Cars had the habit of appearing unexpectedly over rises and tearing down the other side of the road. At night he slept without May Dean, missing fire settling in his own stove, though he lived in dread of the dry season when a spark could set afire, like straw, the shaggy planks nailed together he called home. Once, waiting for sleep, he wondered what strange land Charlie was in, thinking of the morning Charlie had come along the highway in a crowded car and tooted the horn, catching sight of him on the road bank. Charlie had made one signal of good-bye and another meaning what a headache he had, and that had been his final glimpse of Charlie as he tore on north. To a party the night before, May Dean had carried a cake, and others food, and the white boys had brought gallons of wine and he remembered mostly how much laughing everyone had done. The sun glanced off needles of the shiny new pines that morning not as brightly as May Dean's eyes had shone the night before. And she spoke *Par*-tee afterward in a whisper as if it were a word always to be tiptoed around. Remember when we did this at that par-tee, or that, she would say; and the parties they had been to were less than the number of fingers on hands he wished could grab that one and hold it for her always to have. Once he had seen her stop with a clothespin midair, a piece of wash limp on the line, and before inserting the pin, sending a shirt alive in the air, she had been dreaming, he knew, of the party. Charlie had said, shaking hands, "I don't know whether I'll ever see you again or not. Look for me when you see me coming." And that much later the thought of good-bye kept his eyes open and staring into the dark. In the morning, he had told the foreman he wanted to go home.

May Dean, in the plum-purple skirt, was hoeing a garden. He had caught a ride from town and she turned, as country people do, toward the car's sound; gravel flying bounded off things like ice being chipped, and dust floating out and upward settled like low clouds over the flat land; then she saw him, without surprise. He wondered, getting out of the car, what had surprised her in a long time except knowing Charlie.

He brushed away with empty hands mosquitoes humming up from wet ditches along the road, persistent as his thought, and realizing May Dean was never expectant, he thought that was good; she would not be disappointed there was no new skirt.

The state took him on setting out pines along the road banks and still he had to pay a dollar for his ride to town. But he liked working again with something that was going to grow. It was a need a farmer never got over. His fingers deep in dirt, setting upright the tender trees, he imagined them grown tall and thickly together, holding back the road banks, sheltering the highway from the surrounding fields, and knowing he would be an old man then, or dead, made him wonder what it meant to have lived.

On record it was the wettest spring anyone could remember: "wettest and worst," he said, repeatedly sloshing in boots down to the crossroads. Tornadoes were all around and nightly they had warnings. Planting, fertilizing, poisoning had been done and from his position along the road, resodding where the young trees had washed, he looked over water standing in the fields and knew it had all been done for nothing; farmers might as well have burned their money in the fields. In mid-May the tractors began again, turning open the land hopefully to a spring sun which chose to remain hidden. A ritual, he went to work and came home at the same time, while the tractors droned all hours and sometimes into dark. Still, time lost to rain could not be made up; the farmers would not come out ahead. He saw again his time, little man without machinery, was over; and May Dean, his brother-in-law, everyone said it was good he had quit. But when he took down the green pocketbook and looked at the receipts, he mourned for the years he had put his young manhood into, with nothing to show for it at the end.

[144]

His brother-in-law brought news that fall about the new Government program, urging him to apply. "Training-on-the-job for misplaced farm workers," the director told him. "The program lasts nine months. Three hundred and ten dollars a month. Work four days and go to school for one. Think you can?"

"Yes, I'd like school fine," he said. "I can count and write. But I sure need help reading and spelling."

"Try, you'll learn."

"I believe I can," he said.

Fall meant the children in school again with clothes not right. Tommy, the baby, started in a Head Start nursery school and his own class met early on Tuesdays in the same school. Though some of the classes were mixed, his was not, except for the teacher, a stocky young boy who was waiting to go to the service: Vietnam. Walking together from class one day, Jesse told about having a friend named Charlie, in a foreign land. He felt strongly this young boy, like Charlie, wanted to help him. And he could only marvel, as he had with Charlie, over all the world this boy would see. His concentration was not so much on the brightly colored primer, the same as Tommy would use next year, as on the seamlessness of the boy's face, wondering if he even had to shave; and he remembered his feeling of running not to be on time but to catch up.

Fall days were hot, doors and windows stood open, and the teacher was silent as they listened while, from all over the schoolhouse, children sang, *My coun-tree, 'tis of thee, sweet* (their voices rising) *land of lib-er-tee, of thee I sing;* but nothing sang in his heart. His legs doubled beneath the small desk, his knees pressed against its bottom, he felt separate as death from the children's voices. His eyes were on colored circles on the paper while the teacher smiled at the children's voices as if to say they were all in this together; until at last the singsong fell like the sighing of wind and the voices were still. "Now," said the teacher, "multiplying, we learned last week, is another form of what?"

Behind him, the gruff voice of a grizzled old man said hesitantly, "Adding?"

"Right!" said the teacher happily, and drawing forward a frame of colored beads, slid them across the thin silver-colored wire, asking hopefully, "If we have one bead and add four more, how many . . . ?" But the flash of purple-green-silver reminded Jesse of paper-thin fish scales, all colors in the sun. Shades were drawn against the heat and the room was dim and warm. Distraught bees hummed in clover in the sparse grass of the dusty playground while he thought how much May Dean wanted to go to school, and of how only one person in a family could be paid to go, and how if they lived in town and she could get a little piddling job, it would make all the difference. She had canned from the garden but that food would not see them through the winter and it seemed every time they went to the store, prices had risen.

"Zero times anything is what?" the teacher said.

"Nothing," he replied.

Gradually the cabin was decorated with Tommy's drawings. "He has to have up everything he brings home," May Dean said. And by them, they told the seasons. Tommy drew cotton fields like soft white mattresses and pages of brown, gold, red polka-dots were falling leaves. His teacher, Tommy told Jesse, said it was not polite to put a toothpick in your mouth at the table, and Tommy showed May Dean how his teacher had said to hold a fork; then the whole family learned the new way. The fall days took Jesse's breath away — the air like spring water as he trudged to the crossroads every morning, the sky blue as jays, he thought, remembering one sky Tommy colored. The cotton had opened and the fields been cleaned and all the days of fall, while the sun made up for its skittish ways, he was indoors learning to be a plumber's helper. Knowing something about pipes already, being familiar with tools, stood him in good stead, he told May Dean. But the closest they came to a turkey that year was the drawing of one Tommy brought home, its black-spread tail covering a page, its red head the size of a pin's.

Winter was brief, but cold and wet. The children, when they were home, kept television going, and he kept just ahead of the payments. Evenings he talked again of when they would be in the Government house and of how May Dean and the chillen could have the little piddling jobs in town which would make all the difference; wouldn't they? He put from his mind May Dean's not answering, while John, Lu Ann, leaving their own lessons, came to help with his. Even May Dean, remembering her own schooling, helped him. She was the one ought to be in school, he said again. Santa Claus heads hanging about the cabin were stuck with cotton whiskers that seemed to molt, and going from door to door, the family ducked beneath drooping lengths of colored paper chains. To have Christmas at all, they had to go into debt. At school, given a calendar, Jesse took it home to mark ahead time until his program would be over. All around, people they knew were without jobs; even some of the factories were laying people off. "Think you'll be able to get a job with a plumber when the time comes?" May Dean asked, and he could only answer, "I hope so."

"Maybe learning in school will help you get some other kind of job, Daddy," John said, and he said, "Maybe it will."

Hesitantly, he marked on his calendar a new year, and thought of the years lost to him that Charlie, the young teacher, his own children still had ahead. Always they had known that $1 \times 1 = 1$, while he had never seen it written down until recently; he had been able to add subtract multiply only when he took a handful of change from his pocket. "What are our days of the week, Mae?" the teacher said when school began again, and he listened to Mae's earnest voice name the days, Sunday to Sunday. "Look at our picture there, Rob. What do you see?" the teacher said, and Rob's voice, growing old, said, "Kitten, corn, apples . . . ," and the long procession of things he eventually saw strung themselves out with difficulty like the weeks of Jesse's life.

At home, he tried to explain his trouble when, as hard as they tried not to, Lu Ann, John, May Dean grew impatient with him over his lessons. "I just couldn't do it if you didn't keep me reminded," he said. "I just have to be kept reminded"; and he tried to explain it was because so much else came between in a week that by the next week, he could no longer remember. It was like having two jobs. And if he could have only one, going to school, he could learn, he believed. Over and over he said, "I believe I could."

I'm going to keep on trying, he promised. Into the dark, lying awake at night, he said that he was going to keep on trying.

But he began to be late at the crossroads. "Hurry, Jesse," the driver would call, impatiently tooting his horn, and he would trot along the red squishy road; spring, as usual, was rainy. Tommy drew long white lines slanting over waiting fields and as the trees bloomed and calves and colts stood wobbly in fields, the tractors dragged away winter's debris, and he began to feel totally opposite from the rest of the world. "What do you use along with your toothbrush, Jesse?" the teacher asked in health class one day, and nothing at all came to his mind; people smiled, stirred in the class with raised hands. "Now come on, Jesse," the teacher said.

"Everybody knows that." But he did not. His mind, over-crowded, had become one solid useless blank like all the years that had gone before. "Toothpaste!" said the grizzled old man behind him and Jesse smiled, shaking his head about himself, and the teacher said, "I don't believe you're getting enough sleep, Jesse. You look tired."

The word was like rain to crops burning up. As much as he could, he had attended to his plumbing work but occasionally missed a day. Now he said he was tired, just tired. May Dean made him spend two dollars having his blood checked. But believing in nothing was what made him tired. Rain had soaked the cabin floor, thunder shook things from shelves, and spring hail like hen's eggs had bounded off the tinny roof and even when his seeds, fertilizer, poison had washed into the red roads, as sorrowfully as money burning, he had known things would change. At some time, the fields would dry, and dust, rising upward like ghosts, would float over the land, then he would pray for rain as previously he had cursed it, and it would come in time: like a good year after a bad. Seasons repeated themselves dependably, as al-ready along the highway the little pines had grown. But his life stretched ahead blindly now, like hills in the road, and he could not see past obstacles. Summer-laden trees met over-head, darkening the once bright road into a cavern, and the tree roots reached out as he hurried by; and increasingly the driver was calling, "Hurry!" At dusk, when he went back over the road alone, the roots seemed to wait. Each evening he went more slowly as more slowly May Dean's eyes turned to meet his. At home, there were his schoolbooks and John and Lu Ann coming away from their own to help him. "What's this page, arithmetic?" he said, and Lu Ann replied wonder-ingly, "Of course, Daddy." May Dean, he thought, might be better off on welfare without him.

"What are our days of the week again?" the teacher said, in review. Again shades were drawn against the sun and heat wavered the blackboard.

"Sunday," he said. But as hard as he tried he could not name seven. To him, it seemed not to matter, but the teacher looked disappointed. Whatever had happened had happened too long ago, Jesse thought, abandoning hope as once, taking the white man's two dollars, he had abandoned pride. The old feelings fit comfortably; he put them on again, struggling to free his knees from beneath the child's desk, and scratched the name Tommy on top. That's the mark I leave on this school, he thought.

"Quar-ter," the teacher said. "R. I want this class to have learned at least two things. R, not r-uh; and not to put an s on feet. Jesse, how do you spell *penny*?"

Feeling the class wait, he heard them breathing and said, "*P-i-n-e*," but someone laughed; was this the year there had been one cone of cream for seven kids and a penny left?

"That's not quite right, Jesse," the teacher said. "But you got the sound. Try again."

But he would not. "Mary Lou, you spell *penny*," the teacher said and the class went ahead. The day dragged. Bees in clover hummed slowly. The clock hands stood still. Then the final bell rang and, opening his eyes, he saw that while he had slept, time had moved ahead. But the car was not at the meeting place. Surprised, he saw the street empty. The sun stood away, sinking. He remembered leaving the school and walking past streets and corners, turns and shops he had not seen before; but accustomed to moving in a strange world he had not thought, until now, that wherever he was, he should not have been. Now the car was gone. Walking, he thought it was like the time when he left the weighing station, in debt; and he held open the door for the white man's wife to come inside. An instant she had raised her eyes to his; then both had lowered their heads. He had lingered briefly on the platform, hearing through the door cracks. "What's the matter with Jesse?" she had said. "He looks unhappy."

"Unhappy," the boss man had said. "He's got a little change in his pocket and some clothes on; that's all a nigger needs to be happy. 'God's chosen people,' that's what I call them, they're so happy. You've seen them in town on Saturday afternoon."

Then he had gone down off the platform and on into the cold afternoon that now was warm and over these same roads that then had been slippery with ice and now were dusty and worn through the gravel to two slick tire tracks. On either side tangled kudzu vine, looping over telephone poles and trees, was white with dust. Rabbits scurrying out of his way buried themselves in it along the road banks; fields rowed up bore the first hints of cotton, green bursting up out of ground that needed rain. And it was none of his nevermind; working May Dean's garden was all he had to do with any patch of land and he was glad, he told himself. He passed diverted fields a man was paid to let lie and fields that seemed empty, though soon soybean shoots would poke through; vetch was purple, wheat yellow in pastureland; cows grazing raised solemn eyes, chewing, and gazed after him as he passed. On welfare, with groceries every week, the children could keep their bellies full. Ahead, there was a rise in the road cut through a dirt hill; on either side crumbly yellow cliffs rose. It was dark sunk down in the roadway. Always he had been in a hole and able to see no farther than the top of that hole. Now somebody had told him, "Come out"; but the climb was too long if you were worn out when you started. He could go a different way at the crossroads and a long way off from these hills, across bottomland to the highway and from there north or south, either way; just leave out, he thought; the way a white man expected a colored man to do. It would be easier, after all, that way, in a white man's world. He stood, the child's schoolbook rolled up in his hand. He could stick it deep into the kudzu and, like him, it would never be found. Tadpole in a little muddy pond thinks that's it; now somebody had told him different, and he wondered if he was glad. Above this sunk place in the road evening was brighter, and he started up the rise in the road, slapping the child's book against his thigh. At the top he looked down at the cabin; weeds grew its height along the road. It ain't no count, he thought, but inside May Dean was cooking. Smoke rose from the chimney, a thin banner drifting toward the place he was born: two miles away across a field; he never had lived much farther from it than that. It seemed he saw his whole life and knew everything he could: All you can do is wait and see what will happen in the end. May Dean wanted the cabin papered and he thought, starting home, he would get to it, room by room, as soon as he could.

Vistas

.

*T*HE telephone had begun to ring almost daily at five. This afternoon, she decided abruptly, I just won't answer; then she put a hand to the receiver timidly. Amy stared at herself in a dressing-table mirror opposite, where she looked peculiarly elongated, as the mirror slanted. Why, she wondered, had she not been able long before middle age to cope with a telephone call from her mother?

Stretching the cord to its utmost, saying "Hello," she went over to peer more closely at her reflection. Had the apricot oil purchased in the health-food store made her look younger? In only ten days' time, the label had promised. She had questioned Andrew, her husband, explaining the situation; what did he think? This morning she had gazed at him speculatively, saying maybe she had rubbed a bit hard around the eyes and had reddish marks. Andrew, after cocking his head appraisingly, had said, "You look ten days younger." His lips barely twitched.

Now, touching one cheek, she thought, But hasn't it helped, maybe a fraction?

Meanwhile she had been answering the barrage of questions she dreaded. She took a deep breath and, hating to lie, said she had not gotten to the phone sooner because she was in the bathroom. "No, the dishwasher wasn't running. I heard. I was just in the bathroom." She went on wearily to answer that she had had enough dirty dishes to run it last night; and it did take a long time to fill the machine when there were only two people at home. "I will get used to it," she said defiantly, closing her eyes to gaze in inward darkness at fiery red stars bursting. She stood in a right angle between windows and looked out at their separate views. She prayed there might be something else to talk about besides minutia. She burst out: "I did not say I was lonely." Even now, after so many years, she was bound by the conventions of her upbringing, her generation: not to talk back to your elders. Not to say what you thought, Amy added. Her mother was having more of an adjustment problem than she; Amy felt she had been preparing herself for years for the time when her youngest would go off to college; preparations her mother could not fathom. She said evenly, "I know that you had to adjust, too, to my going away from home." She let out an exasperated breath, but away from the receiver.

Her ear ached, and she rubbed it while she went on listening. Far beyond the windows a mock-orange sunset was disappearing, and the ceiling was dabbled by lavender shadows as she stared across a hallway to two tidy, empty rooms that were side by side. She thought suddenly how much better they had looked messy. She wondered about the young mother who had stormed about them crying, "Clean up! Pick up!" Had it so mattered? If only the boys were here at that age, they could begin all over again. Twenty years there had been children in this house, and twenty years had been an instant. She wondered where she had been all that time.

She listened without comment to the latest developments in the various illnesses of her mother's friends. She heard which days her mother had been invited to play bridge. "Thank

[156]

God," Mrs. Howard always said. But Amy was thinking about having two boys in diapers at the same time, a year and a half apart, and how that had equaled four girls, or four of anything else: chimpanzees even. Those early years she had thought that she would never be rested again, that never again would the hackles of her nerves lie flat, that never would she be unharried enough that she was not capable of tossing a tricycle in the general direction of a two-year-old, demanding one minute to herself: carefully avoiding him but putting a nasty hole in a plaster wall, over which she had put a Band-Aid; as she had not been able to explain to Andrew at the time, she had not come up with an answer yet, except that in that period of her life, the Band-Aid had seemed logical.

"Well," Mrs. Howard said, "I suppose we've said everything there is to say."

"I suppose so," Amy said.

"I thought I might drive over tomorrow afternoon." Then into the silence, she said, "Are you doing something then?"

Amy's mind fled this way and that, and settled on the fact that she might do no more than lie on the bed and revel in silence. "I'm working on a paper." Then she said in measured cadence, "I know you think taking a graduate course is silly." She could not say further, "But you see, the difference is that all these years I've been trying to use my brain." Therefore, she assured herself again, she was prepared for this new stage in her life. Why have her mother drive over from a neighboring town? Hadn't they just agreed that everything had been said? To meet, they would only say the same things again; sit avoiding one another's eyes in the silences that fell. Amy would stand at last to make tea, waiting with folded arms while the water boiled, her back carefully to the other room, and she would rattle the dishes to make noise, as she had as a child at meals to disrupt silence between three people at a table, bound by family ties but nothing more. "I have to get the paper done," she said. "Don't come too early. Maybe you had better come some other time, later." Having hung up and lying against the headboard, she could not remember an entire day to herself, without interruption.

The wind must have risen. A sycamore beside the house was scratching at a window, asking either to be listened to or let in. Its bending caused shadows in the hallway to rise and flee, or to shift and resettle; for an instant, she saw several as white mice. The boys had of course that period of white mice; only, her boys set loose a cageful in the house. Where the mice had lived, week upon week, no one ever knew, nor where finally they all had gone; only at unsuspecting moments did they go scuttling across floors from one hiding place to another, escape artists all. One had come out of a closet in a room where she had been writing a novel; it could not be a simple mouse; this one circumvented her toes, with a homemade dart wobbling out of its side, made of a whittled matchstick with a needle imbedded in one end. She had not screeched about the mouse, nor even at acceptance of inherent male bestiality in her own sons; she had quietly rested her forehead on the typewriter keys, thinking about people all over America shut into rooms writing novels that wrenched their very entrails; she had asked them all a simple, heartfelt question: Is anyone else out there writing under these conditions? Once again she had thought about freedom.

Amy felt she had been quite a good mother about white mice; sitting in the dark and recalling, she began to have a great sense of warmth. As her thoughts lodged backwards with the children, she thought that consequently theirs might be lodging back toward home. All this time, in separate New England colleges, they might have been gazing at a similar sunset, then darkness, remembering that when the wind rose, the sycamore scratched at the window, how shortly car lights would come glancing round the school-bus corner and their father would be home, how she would begin to clatter about the kitchen, proclaiming darkly about the lot of women in life and endless meals to fix.

Amy settled upon the child with whom to mull all this over simply by deciding, first, upon the oldest. He spoke thickly but she only said, "How come a girl answered your dorm phone?"

"She lives here," he said.

"Oh," she said. "You sound funny."

"I was asleep," he said.

"Why are you asleep at this time of night!"

"I had a test and stayed up all last night to study."

"You shouldn't do that," she said. "It's not good for your health."

"Mom," he said.

"Are you taking the vitamins I sent you?"

"I'm taking the vitamins. I'm having a poo every day. I'm twenty-one years old. I can take care of myself. What's wrong?"

"Nothing's wrong," she said. "I was just looking at some shadows and they looked like white mice. I wondered if you remembered . . ."

"Where's Dad?" he said.

"He's not home yet."

"You got to get yourself together," he said.

"I am together!" she said. "I just have memories."

"Mom," he said. "I got to run. Or I'll miss my ride to dinner."

"Oh. All right. Good-bye."

"Good-bye, Mom," he said.

"I love you," she said.

"Yeah," he said.

After a moment, Amy dialed with the eraser of a pencil. "Mother, come out tomorrow," she said. "Come for lunch."

Daylight Come

SHE got a job, the first one that was not cleaning house for a white lady. Then something happened. One day her daughter who still lived at home called to say June Bug was not right. My baby! The words started to Scoot's mind. That moment, she was staring into the motel's shiny mirror, in her hand the rag that had polished the glass, along with a little spit. "What the matter with him?" Scoot heard her own voice like a high squeak.

"I don't know, Muh. He acting crazy. You come home."

Home; Scoot let the word echo in her head. Go home? That was exactly what she'd been afraid Lean would want; that was exactly what she'd imagined when she came here, Scoot thought, that this little job couldn't last. It took only moments for everything to go through her mind, though it seemed a long while that she stood looking at her hand holding the receiver, looking into the mirror, hearing Lean breathing on the other end of the line. Scoot's fingernails were short, and so tough she didn't think you could bend them with a hammer; they were dark yellow and almost orange, the color of the old Octagon soap she'd used scrubbing clothes on a washboard for long, long years in a life that was now gone. She had no time to breathe relief over that past being done with.

[163]

Maybe her fingernails were worn down forever, because they had never grown long, so that she could shape them pretty, the way she had hoped to. Also, in this new job, she had to use cleaning stuff new to her, and strong enough to eat down her nails — but she was glad to let them go. Because she had much rather be out of her house at last, out in the world working and seeing things and having her little paycheck to spend. Was it all going to end? She said, "Lean, if I ask for time off to come home when I ain't been here but a week, I'm liable to lose this little job."

There was only Lean's breathing on the other end of the line, and a silence that asked what she was supposed to do. Scoot clenched her nails to her palm, and pressed her feet steadily to the floor, as if to hold on to where she was. "Where he are and what happened to him?"

"Were at the washeteria." Lean's slow voice always made Scoot think of something like a train's whistle, far off and lonesome-sounding in the countryside. It quickened only a little when Lean went on: "A boy called from out there. Said June Bug were acting crazy. Had run out into the highway and almost did get hit. Then just kept running till some boys hanging round grabbed him. I walked and got him."

"Crazy in the head and you walk him home in this heat!" Scoot having spoken almost to herself heard Lean give the only answer she could: "How else are I going get him here?" she said. For once, Lean's voice rose to a sharp little peak. Again there was the thud of waiting silence, with Lean trying to will Scoot home, and Scoot trying to decide what to do. She had raised five children and knew things happened that seemed scary then blew on over. Maybe June Bug was acting out because she'd started leaving home all day for the first time. Even while Lean was on the phone, maybe he had gotten all right. In the background, behind Lean's silent waiting, her light breathing, television went on and on, till Scoot said, "Lean, if nobody looking at that TV turn it off. Go see how June Bug are now." Probably imagined it, but thought she heard the padding away of Lean's bare feet over the living-room's linoleum, because she knew the girl never wore shoes in the house. She knew exactly how everything there looked, too. The sound went down, but not all the way, as if the set were trying to fool her. Who paying all the bills! Scoot cried silently, hoping the set might turn itself off, in sympathy. Then she stood waiting, waiting to know a lot more than what was wrong with her baby, thinking how hard times would be to pay out on the TV if she had to quit working. When the receiver slid from its rickety table once Lean set it down, Scoot imagined it dangling on the end of its cord, the way she was left hanging.

Hope rose as Lean came back; Scoot listened to the scrabbling sound as Lean brought the receiver back to her ear.

"He still crazy, Muh," Lean said. "He in there with the shades all down. Say he never going outside again."

"Crazy from the sun," Scoot said. Hadn't she fallen out from the heat one time herself? She fell out from it in a cotton field when she was picking and was pregnant with her first baby; now, while Lean talked, Scoot thought about that other time.

Lean said, "He wasn't in the sun but to go to the highway. Never acted crazy from the sun before. Ain't but June no how." In Lean's suddenly excited voice, Scoot heard some hidden words: *Sound to me like you crazy too, old woman.*

"Muh, I got to go see 'bout my babies. Like to drive me crazy."

Drive you crazy! Scoot thought. *It's a wonder I ain't white-headed.*

Then Lean hung up after saying, "Muh, you coming?"

[165]

Are I? Scoot wondered. She stared again into the brightened mirror at the person she had become, someone she did not want to lose sight of. Before going out to look for her little job, Scoot had had her head dyed blond by Lean. "Ideas young peoples have today just tickle me," Scoot had said. With her head in the washbowl, she had felt like an Easter egg when Lean poured on yellow liquid. Was it too much foolishness though? she had wondered that day, suddenly a little fearful of feeling carefree. She had raised her head. "Back in my day young peoples didn't have money for nothing. Not nothing!" she had repeated. When Lean's face only looked longer and darker, Scoot said to herself, "She think I'm older than I'm is." Being forty did not feel so old. She remembered, though, how bored she used to be listening to her own mother's tales of being a girl; the time had seemed too long ago to think about; what her mother had been seemed to have nothing in the world to do with the person Scoot had become; yet, the day came when she saw a connection. And Lean in time would see one between them, too, she believed.

She imagined, staring in the mirror at her blond-headed self, who was growing a little large, that Lean would tell her own chillen 'bout back in her day, and suppose she said, "Muh, how come when June Bug went to the highway and almost got kilt, you wouldn't come see after your baby?"

And "How come?" Lean's little chillen might ask, with big old eyes staring in their heads.

After storing her cleaning equipment in a plastic case, Scoot gave a last pat to the room's dresser, having been admiring it when Lean called. Not only had she admired it, but with her new paychecks starting, she had gone out, when the motel's owner passed, to ask how much furniture like that would cost. She had at her house only a puny dresser. Mr. Vas was a nice man, who said he did not know the price, but he could find out from a discount house in Memphis that handled motel furniture. His wife was nice too, though she was always cooking something that smelled funny. Now, a look in Mr. Vas's eyes and something in his helpful manner made Scoot realize he and his wife had come to Mississippi looking for a better life than where they had been, India; though where was that?

She thought of the dresser with affection, having called it "Big'un" from the beginning. Saying good-bye to it now, she looked around the room wishing there were some mark that made the place her own. All she could do, though, was clean up as good as she could, so that Mrs. Vas would want her again. That one straightened room looked just like another one gave her somehow a lonesome, funny feeling. She tilted to the correct angle lampshades that had gone crooked when she dusted, and socked up pillows high as a cat's back on the pretty, tightened bedspreads. Going to the door, she felt as barefoot as Lean, because her feet made no noise on a carpet thicker than any she had ever seen. She stood with the door open, pretending that she was a traveling person, and that her cleaning case was a suitcase and she had come here to spend the night and pay all these high prices!

Closing the door, she was aware last of the smell of lemon oil. Mrs. Vas would know which rooms Scoot had cleaned only because she had assigned room numbers and names from a chart; the morning seemed another life to Scoot now. It seemed to have happened to somebody else. A football team had spent the weekend here; when she and another maid, Candy, arrived today, Candy had said, "Celebrated, I guess!" Scoot had known nothing about a football team before, but now could tell anybody the mess one made. She had learned many things in a short time.

Already, even if it was only June, a curtain of heat like

[167]

colored raindrops danced in the air. Thinking about the twelve rooms she had cleaned today, Scoot leaned against black iron banisters as she went downstairs, tired to the bone. Dragged behind her, her mop's head nipped at her heels like a feisty dog. She was thinking, too, about leaving air-conditioning, when she glimpsed Candy through a room's window and stopped to call. "I got to go home. My baby sick."

"Is?" Candy came out quickly. She was wiping round and round an ashtray, and her eyes set deep in her large face said, Fixing to ask for time off when you just started working here?

"My baby sick," Scoot repeated in a flat, firm voice.

Candy set the ashtray and her dustrag down on a chair, saying, "I'll carry you home then and come on back."

They seemed to fly along the concrete floor and past the black iron railing toward the office, where Mrs. Vas stayed. Candy's big legs in Supp-Hose looked like sausages in their casings. She had advised Scoot to wear them to work, but she had refused. They belonged, she felt, on someone much older, the way Candy was. Suddenly, she thought that not wearing them was a kind of fighting: for things not to happen that you didn't want, as long as you could. She'd better get off the weight she was carrying too, or she'd be looking like Candy.

Running in, Scoot called, "I got to go home. My baby sick," and scared the fire out of Mrs. Vas who dropped a bunch of reservation cards.

"Baby? I didn't know you had one, Louise."

Candy stood panting. "June Bug her baby. But he ten."

"Well, if you think he's sick enough, you've got to go." After hearing their plan, Mrs. Vas said, "We're not going to fill up on a Monday night. Candy, you don't need to come back. You can both finish up tomorrow." But her dark eyes held a little expression that said, if you are reliable. While

[168]

Candy went back to close up the room where she'd been, Scoot started out to the car, thinking of Mrs. Vas's hair as dark as a raven's wing and about her cheeks that seemed natural-born pink. Starting work here, Scoot had told her family, "Peoples running that motel almost dark as we is." Mrs. Vas had said not to call them Mr. and Mrs., but Tony and Pratina. Scoot had not yet worked herself up to calling white people by their first names; it was the first time she'd ever been asked to. Memory was a darkish place with yellow stars; in there was one thing she best remembered her Momma preaching — how to talk to white folks.

The car's windows had been up, and both Scoot and Candy squealed sitting on the hot seat. Then Candy shot them off, spewing red gravel: down off the slope by the highway on which the motel sat; all around the red-dirt countryside looked clawed, for the motel was the first thing built out here, and more things were to come: a whole new shopping center. Out this direction from town was where everything was moving, and Candy sped on toward Scoot's, on the other side of town. With surprise these days she viewed narrow streets. Back in what her chillen kept calling "your day," town was always crowded, Scoot was thinking. Now it was summertime and nobody was outdoors playing. Everybody stayed inside in cool houses and looked at television; at her house they stayed under a fan. Still, she'd go outside with a chair and sit in the yard, but there was not anybody to visit with anymore. Maybe that was another reason she'd wanted to go out to work, just to see somebody else besides the peoples she lived with. Back in my day, she thought, some things was better than they is now.

While talking to herself, she had nodded her head. She and Candy seemed already to be carrying on a conversation when Candy popped out a question. "You got a husband?"

Scoot, not having known Candy before they rode together, had felt her bursting with unasked questions these past few days. "Had one," Scoot answered. "But me and him been separated."

When she stared out at the hard-ridden street, down empty side ones they passed, and at the one main street of town where nothing ever went on, she felt a world of time in which Candy could ask questions and go on waiting for answers, and Scoot decided to tell everything.

"Married fifteen years," she said. "Lived out in the country all that time." She saw again the shaggy, plain, gray cedar house: as clear as if she lived there still. Back in that house wind came through cracks in the walls and floors to rattle oilcloth ruffles she tacked to the edges of boards that were shelves, and made frisky everything else in the house that would move; nothing she could do ever made it pretty. The thought faded as she said, "Then one day Lish took off. Went on up to Memphis."

They might be the oldest friends when Candy said in a soft voice, "Had him sombody else picked out," as if she knew everything already and was not asking a question.

Because she know mens, Scoot thought abruptly. "Had him somebody else picked out," she repeated. "Sho did."

Candy made a little sound that was *ummm*, that went with the sound of the tires over hot tar pavement, shimmering ahead with colors as if oil had been spilled. Then Candy put into words all that her low sound meant.

"That the way mens do," she said. "Quit they wife for another woman."

She been there too, Scoot thought. "Carried off everything me and my chillen had too, but a bed and a chair."

"Give it all to that other woman," Candy said.

"Give it *all* to her!" Inside herself Scoot made a slight screech.

[170]

"What I hated was, he carried my freezer. And it almost paid out on. I hated losing that freezer. Won't never have nare 'nother one."

She felt so much the quiet silent sympathy of the older woman that Scoot had to set her straight, quick. She turned saying, "I never ast him for nothing back neither. Not nothing! I had wanted to get off from that man. Drank up everything us had. Come home so mean I had to run hide out in the cotton field. Sometimes I had to sleep up under the house." She laughed. "Me and the dog be sleeping up under the house together."

"Girl, how come you stay with him so long?"

"Scared," Scoot said. "I wasn't but thirteen when I married Lish. Then had these five babies. And wasn't nothing but a baby myself."

"I reckon." Candy had lit a cigarette and blew smoke from between orchid-colored lips.

The smoke drifted like a streak of gray dust past Scoot's nose and out the car window; its look and scent reminded her of those past days when she built fires outdoors and did her washing by boiling clothes in a black iron pot. She remembered standing in the smoke and the heat to stir round the clothes with a pole, watching the smoke drift off over fields as if it were searching another place to land. "I used to think about leaving Lish. I told him I was."

"I bet I know he told you you ain't going," Candy said. "Mens might not want you, but ain't nobody else going have you, either."

"Lish would tell me, You ain't got sense but to stay right where you is," Scoot said. "Would say, You ain't got sense to take keer your chillens. You ain't got sense to pay house rent. You ain't got sense enough to get a job."

"Well," Candy said, patting Scoot on one knee, "you come out the cotton field and you ain't supposed to know nothing."

"You talking now." Scoot grinned again. "Back then we didn't go nowhere but to the field and back to the house, to Sunday school and church and back to the house."

"Sho how it was," Candy said.

"I used to walk all over that house where us lived." Scoot wrapped her arms to herself, squeezing hard as she'd done then. "Talking to myse'f when Lish be gone fishing. I ain't got sense enough to pay house rent. I ain't got sense enough to take keer my chillens. Ain't got sense enough to get a job. That's how I would go on."

"Well, seem like you doing all right since he left all yawl."

"I have did better!" Scoot jumped round on the seat. "Carried all them chillens into town and some them got jobs and I worked for a white lady. Twelve dollars a week. That what she give me. But that little twelve dollars it hoped me then." That was when June Bug was too little to know she was gone from home, and her oldest girl Little Sister had been there to see after him. Those were the days before Medicaid, too, and she took the job when Little Sister got pregnant, to pay on her baby. Scoot remembered how she had said, "Little Sister, you done messed up, girl."

"We going to get married," Little Sister had said.

Then didn't she tell her what had come to pass: "I bet you my life he don't marry you, you laying out with him all night." Because she knew more about mens by then, Scoot thought.

Though didn't it take Little Sister another baby before she believed her? That how young peoples is, Scoot told herself, remembering how she'd been hardheaded and run off with the twenty-five-year-old black man Lish had been back then. Now Little Sister had a job, tiresome as sewing at that shirt factory was, and had herself a nice government project house, so there was a happy ending. Candy spoke as if she knew Scoot was dwelling on her children. "Where all your chillens are?" she said.

Scoot ached again when she told about the boy who drowned some years ago, but spoke with pride about Little Sister. Another girl worked in Memphis and did not come home much. There was Hootchie-boy, who was in the pen. Suddenly, Scoot realized that the black ironwork at the motel, and its concrete walks, had made her think about Hootchie-boy having his trial; the judge waving arms in his black robe seemed to be flapping wings, saying, "How many times you been in this courtroom, Ulysses?" This time Hootchie-boy went to the pen, the way she'd warned him he would if he did not stop that piddling stealing: cigarettes from the 7-Eleven, meat from the Head Start office, and money out of the machines at the washeteria. Then she knew why Hootchie-boy had been on her mind: What was June Bug doing up on the highway with all those big boys hanging out there? "In the pen for nothing but piddling stealing," she finished telling. "When he get out I hope he do better."

"Everybody going to the pen these days," Candy said. "Rather go to the pen than work."

"They sho got some folks down there," Scoot said. "Funny ones, too. Mens with hair long as mine is. Wearing false eyelashes. Hootchie-boy had to fight one." He had learned about all kinds of things there he hadn't known before; one thing she'd hated seeing on visiting Sundays was the white-trash womens coming to see the colored boys, and going off to little houses that were supposed to be for married folks, but weren't. Hootchie-boy had never seen anything like that, either. "They bad," she said.

"Who?"

"Young peoples."

"They sho is bad," Candy said. "High on theyselves."

"Used to was when my Momma had company, I better get on out," Scoot said. "But my grandbabies they going to stay right where you is, look you in the mouth to see what you saying."

"I know what you talking 'bout," Candy said. "Mine's too."

They were at the house then, and Scoot could no longer leave out what she'd not wanted to tell. "He back now," she said, because there was a tall black man underneath a shade tree on a cane chair. He wore a blue-billed cap and black tennis shoes.

"Who?" Candy said.

"Lish." Scoot nodded toward him.

"— let him come back!" Candy could not get out all her words.

"Didn't have nothing to say 'bout it. Come back 'cause he sick." Then Scoot felt good. "That woman quit him too when he got sick."

It was Candy's turn to grin.

"Little Sister took him in. But he come to my house every day. She go to work and he be lonesome. One reason I wanted this little job, to get out the house and way from him again. He don't do nothing but talk 'bout being sick."

Then, "See you," Scoot said, and Candy was driving off. The tires of her car seemed to Scoot to hum on and on, way beyond the time she could really hear them: out, out to the highway again they seemed to be going. Only to be polite she passed Lish saying, "June Bug sick?" and heard his mutter, "Acting crazy." He kept on staring at his feet — he'd never looked her in the eye since coming back. He seemed to her to look raggedy now even when he wore nice clothes. "How you today?" She spoke to the old woman renter on the duplex's opposite side.

[174]

"Doing all right," Edna said.

"Doing all right, then you be doing good," Scoot said.

She slapped shut her screened door similar to the one Edna sat behind. Sitting on her sofa, Sudie and James ate chocolate pudding and stared up with messy faces. Scoot cried, "Lean, come get your nasty babies!" even if her sofa was not like Little Sister's new sectional one shot through with silver threads. Quiet, Lean was in the kitchen eating too. Scoot passed by into the small room off the kitchen where everybody but her slept. June Bug sat against the headboard of the bed he and Lean shared. The room's crinkled paper curtains let in spots of sunlight that lay across the white counterpane. His eyes seemed to be dancing in his head as he rolled them one direction and then another, to catch the sunlight's glance it seemed. "Muh?" he said. Didn't he know her? She found herself going forward on tiptoe.

"What the matter, boy?" And heard in her voice the same high squeak as when she spoke to Lean by phone; a long time had passed; she had lived over her life while talking to Candy.

"Sun getting me," he whispered. He turned to each window, where the curtains let in sunlight round the edges of dark shades, drawn down. It's spooky in here, Scoot was thinking, afraid though to let in light — but then June Bug bent his head. Bent his head to her hand as she reached out to smooth his springy hot hair. Caught in the back was a comb with a large thick handle; forgetting to be worried, she called out in the furious voice she would normally have used: "What you doing with that comb in your nappy head!"

She snatched it out. "Pimping?" she said.

Lean stood in the doorway saying, "He probably found it. He too little to know what pimping is."

"He ain't if somebody tell him. All those boys wear these

combs to mean they pimping. How come he out on the highway with them?"

"How I know where he are? He went outside. He ain't somebody I got to look after like I do Sudie and James" — they were two and four. "Went there," said Lean, " 'cause that where the action is."

Scoot turned back feeling tired, and stared at June Bug's face so changed since she last saw him. His eyes, which were a little popped, seemed larger and their whites were yellowish. He seemed a little old man shriveled to the size of a boy, except that his thin knobby knees, atop which his chin sat, showed his age so truly Scoot's heart ached; if only he never had to get older. He would not answer.

Lish, who'd come inside, had a voice that rumbled low like thunder; sometimes, it seemed to start before he ever said anything. "He got into something. Got into something out on that highway, I believe."

"What he get into?" Scoot cupped June Bug's face with one hand.

"Smoke dope out on the highway," the low rumble went on. "Got all kind of things us don't know nothing 'bout, don't they, Lean?"

"They stay high," came Lean's lighter voice. "Stay high on something all the time."

"Somebody out on that highway give you something?" she said.

June Bug looked around. "Muh, I scared. Lock all the doors."

Lean went to the other rooms to do it. There seemed nobody else in the world but just those right there; no other people but Lean's two babies and the low voice of television talking to them from someplace that was another world. Scoot felt everybody in the room breathing when Lean came back. "How come you go off the street when I told you not to?"

June Bug shrugged and stuck out his tongue.

"Don't be mannish," Scoot wanted to say. "Don't be showing out." But she sensed too much to come: hurts — his calling her names while going on saying "Muh" and wanting to be near; because that was the way things so often worked out. She began to tremble, feeling the question she asked might be her last; that if he did not answer right, he was gone already. "What somebody give you, boy?" she demanded.

"Gimme that comb," he said slyly.

She threw it at him. "You know I ain't talking 'bout that comb. Talking 'bout what make you act crazy!"

He put one finger straight up to his lips, as if thinking or as if he were not going to answer. Then his teeth bit the tip, and he said, "Gimme a cigarette."

"Who at?" she said.

"White boy."

"What white boy? You know him?"

When he did not answer, Lean said, "He don't know."

"You see him, Lean?"

"No," she said.

Scoot said, "How come he give it to you?"

June Bug rolled his eyes at them, grinning. "You want me to open up these shades?" Scoot cried. "You want all the doors opened? Or you want me in here with you till you not scared."

"Gimme it —" then June Bug's mouth went dry. All in the room could almost see his parched throat when he opened his mouth wide, showing his pink tongue; he ran his tongue round seeking wetness. ". . . 'cause he said it was good."

"Give you just one?" Lish said

"Said he'd gimme more."

"If what?" said Scoot, feeling herself grown smarter: how

far she'd come since that time of going to the fields, to home, and to church. She heard his huge whisper.

"If I'd take the change out the 'chines for him."

"What!" she said.

"How you going do that?" Lean said, laughing a little.

But June Bug said, "He'd gimme —" and licked his dry lips, so that it was Lish's voice rumbling, "Screwdriver all you need." Lean was not laughing.

"How come he asked you?" Scoot said.

"He was talking to some colored boys. They told him I had a brother in the pen. Said Hootchie-boy in the pen 'cause of the 'chines. White boy said he bet I could ope them."

"Hootchie-boy tell you how?" Scoot said.

"Showed me."

"You went with him!"

"Reason that white boy wanted me. I'm little. I can get in and out quick-like."

Scoot reaching out slapped the smartness off his face — she could make a mark here, she felt. She watched him refuse to cry, and saw on his face a look that someday could be meaner. "You going stay in this house with me, you going mind," she said. "Here you is scared of the sun. I has to sit in this house with you no matter how long it take. Have to go and quit my job."

"Quit your job?" Lean echoed.

"I'm got to call that woman and tell her I can't work yet."

She sat down on the bed with June Bug, while dark came on. In the kitchen Lean turned on lights and began to cook supper. Shortly, Lish was back in the doorway saying, "Gone" and in the word there was a question: Could he stay?

Scoot smiled, knowing herself a free woman, and said, "Good-bye then," and let his footsteps leaving sound on through her head. Meat sizzled that Lean was beginning to fry; it smelled so good. She and June Bug smiled at one another. When Lish's footsteps died on out, she wondered what it would be like to find a man who didn't drink up everything and wanted to have something. Only if she found one like that would she want another husband. She listened to the familiar musical drip of water from beneath the refrigerator into a pan. She thought how she had been taking care of chillen since she was fourteen, and she better see this one on out.

She thought how no wind blew in through cracks in this house, and that out in the country she'd been afraid of having no walls to call her own. None of her chillen had known a life like she had. The time came when their lives were their own, to do good or bad. Let them chillen go on talking 'bout "back in your day," Scoot thought. She knew her day had not yet come.